scrambled eggs at midnight

SCRAMBLED

EGGS

AT

MIDNIGHT

BY BRAD BARKLEY & HEATHER HEPLER

DUTTON BOOKS

DUTTON BOOKS

A division of Penguin Young Readers Group

PUBLISHED BY THE PENGUIN GROUP

Penguin Group (USA) Inc., 375 Hudson Street, New York, New York 10014, U.S.A. / Penguin Group (Canada), 90 Eglinton Avenue East, Suite 700, Toronto, Ontario, Canada M4P 2Y3 (a division of Pearson Penguin Canada Inc.) / Penguin Books Ltd, 80 Strand, London WC2R 0RL, England / Penguin Ireland, 25 St Stephen's Green, Dublin 2, Ireland (a division of Penguin Books Ltd) / Penguin Group (Australia), 250 Camberwell Road, Camberwell, Victoria 3124, Australia (a division of Pearson Australia Group Pty Ltd) / Penguin Books India Pvt Ltd, 11 Community Centre, Panchsheel Park, New Delhi - 110 017, India / Penguin Group (NZ), Cnr Airborne and Rosedale Roads, Albany, Auckland 1310, New Zealand (a division of Pearson New Zealand Ltd) / Penguin Books (South Africa) (Pty) Ltd, 24 Sturdee Avenue, Rosebank, Johannesburg 2196, South Africa / Penguin Books Ltd, Registered Offices: 80 Strand, London WC2R 0RL, England

CIP Data is available.

Published in the United States by Dutton, a division of Penguin Young Readers Group
345 Hudson Street, New York, New York 10014, www.penguin.com/youngreaders

Designed by Heather Wood
Printed in USA   First Edition
1 3 5 7 9 10 8 6 4 2
ISBN 0-525-47760-8

For my family:
who always believed, even when I didn't
—*H. H.*

For Lucas and Alex and my parents,
with love and gratitude
—*B. B.*

ACKNOWLEDGMENTS

Knowing that this is the place to thank everyone from preschool teachers to friends to the guy at Starbucks who kept giving Heather free refills and even slipping her biscotti every once in a while, we will try to be brief.

First, thank you to Stephanie Owens Lurie at Dutton for wanting this book so much and for her kindness and generosity.

Second, to Peter Steinberg at Regal Literary for finding the best home for this book and for laughing at Brad's stories and introducing Heather to the best chocolate ever.

Third, we are grateful to Sarah Shumway for being organized when we weren't.

Fourth, thank you to Emily Romero and Allison Smith at Dutton for getting the word out.

Fifth, thank you to Rosanne Lauer at Dutton. Without you who knows how many typos there might have been.

Thank you finally to everyone else at Penguin Group and Dutton, including Doug Whiteman, Jennifer O'Donohue, Janet Krug, Gina Balsano, and Erin Dempsey.

Thank you to our friends in Maine, who offered encouragement when needed and criticism when warranted—Kasey Greico McNeally, Elizabeth Searle, Clint McCown, A. Mannette Ansay, Leslea Newman, Suzanne Strempek Shea, and Jan Greico.

And, because this is Heather's first novel, she has a lot more people to thank: Thank you to my friends in Machias, Maine, who encouraged me all the way—Randall Kindleberger, Laurel Robinson, Cindy Huggins, and Linda Patryn. Thank you to Jodi Kearns for her excitement. Thank you my sister, Terry O'Daniel, for making me laugh. Thank you to Lisa Tarr for her creativity and for telling us this book made her cry. Thank you to Bob Hepler for his patience. Finally, thank you to my son, Harrison, for being prouder than anyone else.

scrambled eggs at midnight

My mother is a wench. It says so right on her W-2.

She isn't a very good one, though, and that's why we have to move again. This will be the third move since last summer. Delores had miscalculated, quitting her job before we had enough money to make it through to May. We'd spent until after Christmas in a one-bedroom apartment above a bait shop. The sign hanging below my bedroom window read BAIT SANDWICHES AND ICE GAS, and the smell even in the off-season made me swear off fish for life. We left when the manager threatened to lock up our stuff if we missed another rent payment. All of March we spent in a hunting cabin borrowed from the dishwasher at Whole Earth. We had to move out when Delores set fire to the floor with her soldering iron.

We've been camping out here at the Bluebird Inn ever since. I've been helping Delores get the rooms ready for the summer in exchange for our suite. *Suite* makes it sound nice, but it's really seasonal trash. The addition of a couch and a short wall create our living room. The carpet matches the wallpaper, which matches the bedspread, which matches the stains on the towels, turning everything into Beige World. Even the paintings are of muted beach scenes and dimly lit forests of birch trees.

We pretty much eat whatever we can keep in the mini-fridge or heat in the microwave. Tonight it was organic vegetable soup from a can and hunks of sourdough bread. I do most of the cooking because Delores forgets to eat when she's inspired. She stays hunched over the desk at night, twisting bits of metal and glass into miniature angels or mermaids or fairies. Lately she's been trying some new things, incorporating found objects into her jewelry. Last week for my birthday she gave me a pendant that she made out of a bottle cap. The cap is twisted and folded in on itself, but you can still read the M in MOXIE if you look closely. It's wrapped with filaments of red and orange glass and twisted around with silver wire so that it looks like a folded sun.

Before she gave it to me, she strung it on a piece of cinnamon dental floss. I was mad when first I opened the box, thinking she had no right to go through my stuff like that, taking the cap without asking. But when I glanced over at her, I couldn't stay mad. Sometimes when I look at her I feel like I'm the mother and she's my child, like she's just waiting for me to tell her that I'm proud of her. She looked so small just then that I hugged her and told her thank you. Later in bed I pulled the pendant free from under my shirt and studied it. It really *was*

nice, and now I can wear the cap all the time, so I'll never forget. I fell asleep dreaming of a town in Texas, a wide part in the
road between Nowhere and Where You're Headed. The baked
landscape swirled with dust, which filled my nose with the scent
of cinnamon.

"Moving day," Delores sings from inside the bathroom. I squint
at the digital clock, then roll over, away from the sound of the
shower starting, and pull the other pillow over my face. Maybe
if I just lie still enough, she will go without me. I must have
fallen back asleep because suddenly Delores is right there, her
face just a couple of inches from mine.

"Go 'way," I mumble. I can smell the peppermint from her
toothpaste and the lavender from her shampoo.

"Calliope June," she begins, "either get up or I am going to
get you up." Delores's threats sometimes involve cold water or
loud music, and I'm not prepared to be soaked in either this
morning. I stumble to the bathroom, tripping on a stack of
sweaters on the way.

I stand under the blast of hot water longer than usual. I'm
not sure when I'm going to get another shower. Delores calcu-
lated that the drive from Maine to North Carolina could be
done in two days. Last summer when we drove from California
to here, I only got one shower that whole week, and that one
was either because Delores felt sorry for me or she couldn't
stand my stink any longer. A tuna sandwich past its prime in

Idaho had given me food poisoning, and Delores didn't pull the car over soon enough the first time. We spent the night in a truck-stop motel, where the sounds of grinding gears and air brakes kept us up for most of the night, but it was worth it for the shower and a real bed. Camping out is only fun when you know that after a few days you get to go home and take a bath and flop in front of the television. Whenever we hit the road on one of these trips, I'm never sure what is waiting for us at the other end.

"You're not going to get any cleaner," Delores shouts from the other side of the bathroom door. I've learned to lock her out. "We need to get *going,*" she says. I can almost see her through the door, tapping the toe of her purple Chuck Taylors or twisting her hair into a bun at the nape of her neck. "We can get doughnuts," she calls. She must be getting desperate. I decide to push my luck.

"Lemon filled?" I ask, my hand poised over the faucet. Silence. Finally a sigh and a mumbled "okay." Delores hates fast food, so I know this is killing her. I leave the water running for an extra moment or two before shutting it off. My red hair falls nearly to the middle of my back when it's wet, and I can feel it shedding streams of water down the backs of my legs. I wrap one of the huge towels around me and struggle to pile my hair up on top of my head. I wipe away some of the fog on the mirror before baring my teeth at myself. They are one of my best features, straight and white. I had my braces removed only a couple of months before all of this mess started, back when we still had medical insurance. I can hear Delores bumping around in the next room, and I hurry to get dressed. The last time I left her alone too long, she tossed most of my books in the Dumpster and I spent the better part of an hour knee-deep in garbage trying to sift them all out.

"Try to keep it down to that duffel and one box," Delores reminds me before carrying another box out to the car. As if I needed reminding. Delores has few rules, but one of them is that all that we own has to fit in the car, which isn't easy considering we own a two-door Datsun hatchback.

I push my down vest into the duffel, making the sides bulge.

"You'll never zip it up," Delores says, lifting the red tackle box from the bed. "Can't you leave some of that stuff behind?"

I look over at the mound of jeans and cords that threatens to spill from the top of the dresser. An equally tall stack of books teeters beside it, quivering with some unseen energy. I've made some deep cuts in my inventory already. Delores stands, watching me, as I push two tank tops into my sneakers and change the alignment of my nesting dolls.

"Got it," I say, pulling at the two halves, willing them closed.

"Want some help?" she asks. For her that means helping me get rid of more stuff. I shake my head.

"Suit yourself," she says, carrying a plastic grocery bag full of our bathroom things to the car. I hear her start it up, gunning the engine once to keep it from stalling. I pull a sweatshirt from the top of the pile and yank it over my head. Light one item, the duffel zips easily. I shove my arms into the sleeves, heft the bag from the bed, and take one last look around for anything I might have missed. I pull the door shut hard, hearing the lock catch, and turn toward the parking lot. As I limp toward the car under the weight of my bag, I pray that Delores won't notice that I have on three sweatshirts, one layered on top of the next.

Delores's jewelry business, if you can call it that, used to be named Earthly Delights by Delores. I made her leave off her name and stop dotting the *i* with a tiny peace symbol. "Hippies don't have money for nice jewelry," I told her, "and you'll scare off the real buyers with your politics." Her response was, "Peace isn't political," but I noticed she started finishing the *i* with a regular dot. Boxes full of her stuff take up most of the space behind our seats. The cord from one of her soldering irons has slithered out of its box and flaps against the metal side of one of her rock tumblers. I tuck it back inside before shifting the tackle box under my feet so that I can stretch my legs. Delores has pushed the seats way forward to accommodate all of our stuff. This isn't a problem for her. She's tiny. But I've got my dad's height and already tower over her by nearly eight inches.

"Don't forget we need to stop at a post office today," I say, staring through the windshield. "If we don't get that stuff mailed, we'll have to pay a penalty." I've been trying to get our taxes together, but it's hard when we're moving so much. Delores tells me to forget it.

"It's not like they're going to catch us," she says, and she's probably right, but somehow filling out all the official forms that I picked up at the library makes me feel like I'm part of the system, part of the machinery, not just some random particle bouncing off everything it hits.

"Post office," she repeats, but I know I'll have to remind her again later. "So, what do you want for breakfast?" Delores asks this without turning toward me.

"Don't start," I say.

"How about some nice fruit and maybe some yogurt?"

"Doughnuts," I say. "Lemon filled."

"I know a good organic market in Blue Hill that is only a tiny bit out of our way."

"I know a Tim Hortons that isn't out of our way at all."

"Maybe they'll have organic coffee," Delores says, pushing the button on the radio. Static fills the car. Then jazz.

"I wouldn't count on it," I say, shifting lower in the seat, scrunching up one of my sweatshirts against the window. I lean into the door. One more year and I can drive. Not that I hope we have anywhere to go in a year. Most kids can't wait until their sixteenth birthday so that they can drive away. Go someplace. I'm hoping that by then we won't have to leave. Maybe by then we'll have found somewhere we can stay.

The inside of Tim Hortons smells exactly the way a doughnut shop should. Too sweet with the scents of maple and chocolate and powdered sugar. Delores insists that we go in instead of doing drive-through. "I want to actually *watch* them make my coffee," she says. I stand back as she quizzes the counter girl, asking her how fresh it is, whether it's made from certified organic beans, if they use purified water. The girl looks frightened by the tiny woman in front of her. Delores can be a little intense sometimes.

"What she means to say is that we would like two tall skinny lattes and two lemon-filled doughnuts," I tell her. The girl seems relieved and turns to plunge the heated tip of the frother deep into a pitcher of milk. Delores started on this organic kick right after she left my father. She told me she was trying to detoxify her life. No chemicals, no preservatives, no artificial enhancers, no dyes. We eat free range, all natural, certified, 100 percent pure, nothing added. One thing about Delores is that whenever she makes her mind up about something, it stays made up. No matter what. Even on that first drive from Texas to Des Moines, I can remember stumbling behind her in tiny markets scented with patchouli and overgrown with wheatgrass, filling our basket with things I had never seen before. Tofu, miso, kale, sprouted-wheat bread. It was lucky I couldn't eat anything then.

We drive down the coast, squinting into the sun and shivering in the cold air swirling in through the broken back window. "It'll be warmer in North Carolina," Delores says, as if that could be enough to make me look forward to the summer. I hold the spiral-bound Rand McNally in my lap, flipping pages as we pass through each state. We slip through them, five in one day, too fast to get more than a brief sense of them. Maine seems populated more by trees than by people. Stone buildings huddle against the rivers in New Hampshire. Giant warehouses advertising state liquor stores flank the highways in Massachusetts. Connecticut will forever stay in my mind as the place with the truck stop where I had the best piece of lemon pie ever and a man exposed himself to me while I waited outside the restroom for Delores to come out.

Sometimes when I'm waiting like that, I have to fight the urge to go find her. When I can't see her, sometimes I wonder if she's just disappeared again. I've gotten to the point where I keep the keys when we stop. I tell Delores it's because I am afraid she'll lose them, but it's not that. If I have the keys, she can't drive away.

We push through until we find a campground with full facilities just inside the border of New York. Too tired to even change, I crawl into my sleeping bag without taking my clothes off. I feel Delores shift once before she presses her back against mine, trying to find warmth in the cold air. It's the first time she has touched me all day. That too had changed on that rainy Saturday in Texas. While trying to rid herself of chemicals, preservatives, and my father, she had also lost something else. I still hug her sometimes, like when she gave me the necklace, but it seems to hurt her when I do. Like something about the way I touch her burns her skin.

I sigh into my sweatshirt, trying not to wake Delores. She's already edgy, snapping at me for accidentally pumping the wrong gas, popping my gum too loud, and even once for sighing. "Calliope, sighing isn't going to make it not so." Maybe not, I think, but it makes me feel better. I sigh one more time before twisting my sweatshirt around my neck to keep warm. I only have two wishes for tomorrow. The first is that Delores's boss won't be a jerk like the last one, thinking that wenches are actually prostitutes with long dresses. The second wish is that there will be somewhere nice for us to live. Two summers ago we got to live in a bed-and-breakfast owned by one of the jousters. I'm not hoping that high, but something other than our tent might be nice. There is a third wish, but it's one that I have carried for too long to even let myself think about. It's not fully formed, a vague sense of wanting something or someone or somewhere. I don't let myself try to figure it out. I just push down into the flannel of my sleeping bag and close my eyes. Tomorrow things will be better, I think. Tomorrow we'll be there.

The letter was printed on paper with a watermark of a shield and crossed swords. This should have been enough to make Delores think twice about taking the job, but she was determined. "We need the money," she said, and I thought, *Thank you, Dr. Obvious.* "Besides," she continued, "I'll bet they'll hire you this year." Like that was just the thing to seal the deal. I sigh and stare out the window. Delores estimates that we will be in

Asheville in under nine hours. The fairgrounds are only about ten minutes beyond that.

"It's the oldest Renaissance Faire in the country," she says. I know enough about this after four years to mentally add the *e* to *fair*. I've found that you can make just about anything Old English if you just add a letter or two. Four summers of Faire and I still can't quite get my mind around grown people dressing up in tights and corsets and pretending to live hundreds of years in the past. Some people, like Delores, count on it as their primary source of income. Others are part-timers. Those are the worst. It's as if they have to cram a year's worth of bad behavior into three or four months. They start fights in the name of chivalry. They bump into women, offering them a grope as a way of complimenting them. They get drunk almost daily, wanting to find that peaceful agrarian way that they must assume is at the bottom of the next mug of mead. You can spot the part-timers easily. They are the ones that have a cell phone stuck into the pocket of their vestments or a Timex hidden under their leather wrist cuffs.

Delores is all about authenticity, except in one crucial area. She is a feminist. That might not be such an issue in modern society, where people are forced to bend over backward in the name of equality; but at Faire women are either ladies or whores, and Delores isn't much of either. She does fine in our own booth, selling her jewelry. It's the refreshment tent that gives her trouble. She discovered quickly that she couldn't make enough money just selling necklaces and rings, so she got herself hired as a wench. It's pretty much like it sounds.

"There'll be a phone there," Delores says, without looking at me. I know even this much is hard for her. "We'll get you a phone card." We haven't had a phone in over four months. The motel where we were staying just had a pay phone bolted to the front of the office building. You had to want to make a call pretty bad to stand shivering in the cold. I tried to call twice, getting the machine both times. I didn't leave a message.

"Thanks," I say, trying to make my voice sound normal, but the thought of calling panics me a little and Delores must have sensed this, pulling out something we could both cling to.

"Only if you want to," she says. "No pressure." She pats my knee in what I'm sure is an attempt at motherly affection, but which comes off like she is dusting dirt from my pant leg. Her hand retreats as quickly as it arrived, finding its place back on the wheel. Ten and two they teach you in driver's ed. At that moment, eyes straight forward, hands firmly gripping the cracked plastic, Delores is the picture of a safe driver. Only the nervous habit she has of chewing on her lower lip lets me know that all is not well within.

Asheville is bigger than I expected. And more claustrophobic. After having lived with the Atlantic out my back door for more than eight months, the mountains make me feel like I'm sitting in a bowl with sides that are too tall to climb. I watch as the buildings slither past—coffee bars, used-book stores, art galleries. It seems like parts of San Francisco, but without the water or the atmosphere. People with too much money and not enough to do step in and out of the shops, arms loaded down with expensive coffee drinks, probably made with soy milk, and bags full of books they will never read. Twice I see groups of people my own age: leaning on the side of a building under a sign for organic vegetables, and clustered around a wrought-iron table in front of a coffee shop called Cool Beans. *Clever,* I think. Coffee shops and hair salons are known for their witty names. Idling at a light, I'm aware of someone looking at me from the curb. I turn just as the light changes. As Delores accelerates, I see two things. A T-shirt that reads JESUS IS A LIBERAL and a hand raised either in a hello or in another gesture, one that I am much more familiar with.

The entrance to the Faire is unfinished. The letter stated that opening day is scheduled for May 31, less than a week away. They have a lot of work to do.

"This seems nice," Delores says, rolling our car into the parking lot. Dust dances around the car as she pulls even with a van covered with Celtic symbols. I unfold myself from the car, hearing my back pop in protest as I straighten up. I am going to need some serious yoga to recover from this trip. I step around the back of the car, where Delores has stopped in the middle of opening the hatch. I look to where she is staring and have to squint in the waning sunlight. The van sports Virginia plates emblazoned with the word JOUSTER. I roll my eyes at Delores, making her smile for the first time all day.

"Welcome home," I say, lifting her woven bag from the back of the car.

Finding the check-in tent closed until morning, we return to the car to dig out our tent and sleeping bags.

"Good e'en," a deep voice says as we walk around the back of our car. The jouster sits, his bare feet dangling from the tailgate of his van.

"Good e'en to you, sire," Delores answers, her voice dipping and dancing in the evening air. I always have to bite the inside of my cheek to keep from laughing at the absurdity, two grownups playing make-believe.

"Do you need some help?" he asks, sliding from the tailgate into the sandals that rest on the ground beneath him. He is taller than I thought and older than I expected. Hints of gray thread his brown beard. "The name's Phinius," he says, extending his hand toward Delores. Catching my look, he smiles. "I'm serious. My parents were hippies before their time."

"My name's Delores," she says, sliding her hand out to meet his. "And this is Calliope."

"You too?" The jouster smiles at me again. He smiles too much.

"Call me Cal," I say, finding his hand with mine.

"Well, you can call me Phi," he says, taking the tent from Delores in the midst of her protests. "I'll show you two where to camp." He hefts my mother's bag in his other hand. I see something that I never expected to see. Even in the dim light, I can see Delores's cheeks grow pink as Phi reaches around her to close the hatchback. I busy myself with setting up the tent as Delores thanks Phi for his help.

"'Tis nothing, fair lady," Phi says. "Perhaps I will see you tomorrow at breakfast?" I don't hear Delores's response as I wrestle with the tent stakes. "Well, then," he says, openly staring at Delores, "I will bid you good night." I watch Delores shake her head slightly as she turns toward me. Neither of us says anything. Instead I watch her listen to the faint whistling that eventually grows silent as he makes his way back through the trees.

I fall asleep to the sound of our tent rustling in time with the trees, and with a longing so strong that I can't even say for sure what it is that I'm missing. I can't even say for sure if what I need is something I've had before and lost, or something that I'm still waiting to find. But it's there. An ache deep inside me. A slowly twisting pain that I try to ignore, because it threatens to pull me under if I let it.

2 eliot

I don't like the name Eliot, but I'm stuck with it. And it's not that I don't like the name because I don't like the name, but really it's because the name is based totally on a mistake. I came along about the time that The Dad started finding God, and he somehow thought it was a biblical name. Eliot. I mean, what was he thinking? I say that to him sometimes, and I want to know . . . was he thinking maybe Elijah? Emanuel? Esau? Ezekiel? He doesn't like me to question him. He says it's a sin. Everything became a sin in 1998, when he first opened Sonshine Valley Christian Camp and we moved from Carolina Beach all the way out to the mountains, out to one of the cabins, to a room in the cabin. If they'd put a box in the room in the cabin in the mountains, I probably would have moved into that. Everything got smaller, and I miss the beach. And I mean, I miss it the way you would miss a finger or something. All we have here are cabins and pine trees and two ponds full of geese and lots of geese crap and what The Dad calls our facilities, which just means some showers and a place to eat and the exercise trails. We don't have people; we don't have a town. The cabins are called rustic in the brochure, which is a nice way of saying "really old." But Mom has fixed the camp up pretty nicely, doing all the painting and drywall and wiring. She is good at stuff like that, and The Dad never has been. He's good at numbers. He's good at money.

At first this was just a place for church groups to come to barbecue and play volleyball, and The Dad made a few bucks. Then one summer he had the idea to run this special theme camp called *Get Thin with Christ!* and a busload of fat kids came and prayed and learned to eat salad, then the next summer the same camp, but for adults, and that was that. A business was born. He has written two books already, has been on TV and everything. You've seen his T-shirts, the hats, the rainbow bracelets, the bumper stickers, the billboards, the cookbook— WWJE, *What Would Jesus Eat?* On page 347 is a recipe for salmon with capers, a yogurt-based dill sauce, arugula salad with a balsamic vinaigrette, and a sugar-free mini-cheesecake for dessert. I feel pretty sure that Jesus wouldn't eat that. Or didn't eat that, anyway. But what do I know? I like saying that, because I can pretend not to know everything I know.

What I knew this morning was that I needed to get out of there. Later that afternoon the hunters were coming out again, because of the geese, and I'm no wuss, but I didn't want to see it. I also needed to get out of there because I have a box of arsenic being drop-shipped at the UPS in Asheville, and I have to pick it up. Arsenic and black powder and potassium nitrate. It's not exactly legal for me to have them. The Dad will let me drive into town if I'm picking up supplies for Sonshine Valley, even though I don't even have my permit yet. He says we are operating under God's laws, not man's. But really he just wants me to help out, besides cleaning the cabins. He doesn't know about the black powder and other stuff, and neither does Mom. I charge it to Sonshine Valley and the bill comes in as "Chemical Supplies," and I just say it's cleaning supplies. Bad, I know.

So when I asked for the keys, The Dad looked up from his computer and took a sip of his green tea, the steam fogging the glasses he wears. They aren't real lenses, but when he goes to churches and bookstores and on TV, he wants to look smart, because he tells people what to eat and what not, and he wants to make the Loaves and Fishes Diet sound scientific. It isn't. He used to sell swimming pools for a living.

"Headed into town, huh, sport?" He smiled. His hair is curly, like mine, except turning gray and he dyes it dark, but a shade darker, like he's forgotten what he used to look like.

"Yes," I told him. "Can I take the van?"

"You need to pick up galleys of the new book, right?" He frowned a little, hardly looking at me, and thumbed through the calendar sitting upright on his messy desk, *365 Little Bless-*

ings. He is working on his own calendar, if he can think up 365 things to say about God and fat people.

"That's right, I do need to," I told him. Here is the thing about lying . . . I don't like it. I lie in a way that's not a lie. I tell The Dad I need to pick up his galleys because it's true, I do. I was supposed to three days ago and forgot, and so if he thinks I'm going into town now for that, then I can get the books with my supplies, and it's like it's not a lie. You say things that the truth can fit around, and it feels OK. Except, really, it doesn't. Every time I do it, I feel like I'm inside something and only I know what it is, and I'm alone in there, like I've built this big empty room around myself and there's no door. I didn't look at him much either.

Just then Mom walked in, toweling her hair. She runs five miles a day and then goes over to the exercise room and lifts: back, chest, and arms on odd days, legs and abs on evens. I know the drill. The Dad tells her, I hear him, that they have to look the part.

"Eliot is going into town, if you need something," The Dad said to her.

"I don't like you driving," she said. She unwrapped a Power-Bar and bit into it, the towel draped over her blond hair. The Dad has plans next year for his own power bar, called the Manna Bar. They're rich, did I say that?

"I'll be careful," I told her. True, when you are carrying arsenic and black powder, you're careful.

SCRAMBLED EGGS AT MIDNIGHT

"If you get arrested driving, they will put you *under* the jail," she said. "Us too, for letting you."

"I won't," I said.

"God's laws, not man's," The Dad said, and she turned away a little, frowned, and sighed. More and more she does that, and I think maybe she is just tired, tired of working out, of being perfect, of all the rules. The first book The Dad published was called *Eye of the Needle: Why God Wants You Thin!* You might have noticed, there are lots of exclamation points in the God business. I think that's what Mom is tired of, all the exclamation. Maybe she just wants her life to have a few periods, a few quiet little commas.

I feel at home in the van with the windows rolled down and the stereo turned up and all that warm-bath summer wind blowing in and around and I'm wearing my sunglasses, which look slick the way they hug my face. Think Bono back when he was cool. I hang my arm out the window and thump-thump the steering wheel like I don't care about anything, and for a minute it is easy to forget I'm driving the Sonshine Valley van with the big cartoon cross painted on the side. The cross has these lines shooting out from it, like the sun, I guess, but all I can think is it's how Dagwood or Ziggy or Charlie Brown always look when they get surprised, with lines shooting around their heads. I wish that would happen to me. I want something, someone, to make lines shoot out of my head. Besides the shades, I'm also wearing my JESUS IS A LIBERAL T-shirt. It's kind of a rebellion thing, I guess, because The Dad would hate it, but here's my question—is it rebellion when he doesn't know about it? Can you rebel in secret? I'm thinking not, and I'm thinking I'm pretty weenie about the whole thing because anytime I have it on around the camp I wear it under a hoodie half zipped, so all The Dad or Mom ever reads is JESUS IS. I don't want to make them feel bad. Like just before I left the house, just as The Dad tossed me the keys, he said the same thing he always does, "Be careful, Eliot. I want you back in one piece," only he got quiet when he said it, all jokiness drained out of it, and I could see him thinking about how bad it would be if something did happen to me. He does that, sometimes, gets quiet, and I watch him really thinking about me, a real thought breaks through about me or Mom during those rare times when he's not thinking about money and heaven and cholesterol.

I like the UPS place, because with a drop-shipment I get to walk right into the back, where there is a concrete floor and this stripey yellow tape on it where the trucks are supposed to park, like it's a big aircraft carrier and those clumsy fat brown trucks are fighter jets that have to hit their marks just right or fall off into the ocean. I like that they made everything brown. All part of a plan to lower expectations. Fast things aren't brown. Fast things are red, or bright yellow like lightning. Not brown. So, you send your stuff, and you're thinking slow, brown, slugslugslug, and what happens? Your package gets there the next day and you're like, whoa . . . and I sympathize with the whole plan. Most of my life has been a strategy of lowered expectations. Sometimes I even surprise myself.

I have to sign all kinds of papers because of the arsenic, but they are used to me picking it up, so they don't question me too much. The woman who signs me out is named Gil, which is short for something—I have no idea what—and she is very nice and smiles at me every time. The other thing about brown is that you'd be surprised how good it looks on women, that uniform. Maybe that's just me. I have to back the van into the warehouse, and I have to hit a strip of the yellow tape, and Gil guides me with her hands, like an airport worker. Her nails, I see in the rearview, are painted orange. Brown and orange. I want to tell her she is the same color as autumn, my favorite season, but I don't know if telling a woman she looks like three months out of the year is a compliment or not. I'm thinking not. She tells me I have a burned-out taillight, and then she checks my ID. This always makes me nervous, always. See, the only ID I have besides the Frequent Coffee Club at 7-Eleven is a fake one. It's my picture, it looks exactly like a North Carolina driver's license, but I bought it for $25 out of the back of a magazine. It's sold as "Novelty License, for Amusement Purposes Only," like people are going to sit around looking at it and cracking up. Yeah, right. How it works is, you take a picture of yourself standing in front of whatever color background is right for your state. I looked at Mom's license and it turned out to be dark red. But I didn't have to stand in front of anything, I just filled it in on the computer, the exact shade. You send them the picture and they make the license for your state, and it looks exactly right, except—and I guess this is the novelty part—at the top it says something like "TV Remote Operator's License," or "Skateboard Driver's License," ha-ha. That part is written on this piece of plastic above the top, so when you get it back in the mail, you just take an X-Acto knife and cut that part off.

So Gil takes the license because it's part of her job, and instead of handing it right back, she holds it up, under the light.

"Are you really six feet tall?" she says. Her orange nails look like candy corn.

"I'm tall for my age," I say, and reach for the license. She draws it away from me.

"You're tall for anybody's age," she says. "And a hundred sixty, huh? Somebody needs to feed you a little more."

I nod. "That's kind of an issue around my house," I say. "But the locusts and honey are good."

She laughs, then shakes her head a little, and I wonder how we must look to everyone, if we are the local cranks, along with the guy who always writes to the paper because he thinks fluoride in the water is part of a government cover-up.

"Different hair then," she says. According to the license, I'm eighteen years old. It's like a little plastic time machine, propelling me three years into the future. Sometimes I wish it were a time machine, but then I think, where would I go?

Gil hands the license back to me and smiles, and I breathe again, put the ID away. She is pretty, with brown hair that moves a lot and these crinkles around her eyes, but she is old too, probably thirty, and I know that she flirts with me not because she thinks of me that way, but because she doesn't. I'm safe, a distraction between coffee breaks. The most dangerous thing about me is a van loaded with black powder and arsenic.

OK, about all of that.

I know what most people would think—crazy boy in the basement making pipe bombs, stirring up poison, adding to his list of enemies every day, one of those pale wussies who are a little *too* into their video games. Well, that is so wrong, because none of the cabins even *have* a basement.

That was funny.

No, the thing for me is not making destruction, it's making beauty. Fireworks. The kind like you see on TV shooting up behind orchestras and over bridges and monuments on the Fourth of July, not the crappy bottle rockets and Roman candles that little kids buy. The real stuff—Thunderbolts, Peacock Plumes, Rosebuds, Serpents, Creepers, Saucissons, Whirlwinds, etc. Most people don't know those names, and some I made up, but everyone knows what they look like, all that white and gold and blue exploding into stars, shaking the ground. *Oohs and ahhs instead of applause.* I read that once in some pyrotechnician's magazine. Pretty dumb. A lot of my materials come from the Home Depot in Asheville, others from the craft store. I'm not supposed to be doing this, not any of it. I can't even think about how much trouble I would be in, real trouble, because I'm buying this stuff with a fake ID and I'm too young to have it. The fireworks are considered class-two explosives, and I'm not supposed to even shoot off a charge I *bought*, never mind made, until I'm licensed, and that can't happen yet. Not until I'm eighteen, not until I've apprenticed with a licensed pro. And just where am I supposed to find *him*? I've checked all the cabins; he's not here. But I love it, and I'm not stopping, no matter how far in I am.

The thing about a firework is, you make it, all of it. Like gardening, if you made the dirt and the seeds, the steel for the watering can and the watering can itself, and then you made the water. You spend a week packing a charge, you light the fuse that you rolled until your hands turned black, and the spark crawls its way into the mortars that you cut from plastic pipe, mounted on boards you also cut. The lifting charge sends it into the air; the fuse lights a second fuse. And you have to make everything come out timed just right, working like a machine as it flies up into the air, burning up black powder that's the same as it was in China five hundred years ago. Then the whole thing shinnies up an invisible rope and destroys itself by lighting up in color and fire, better to look at than a thousand paintings or a thousand movies. And then it's gone. Like that, it's over, all your weeks of work. You control it, then you don't, and all you can do is watch and hope it's beautiful.

This is my thing. It's what I want to do, what I'm going to do. Some people get to be forty and never have their thing. I do one show a year, a small one out over the goose pond at the end of fat camp. My parents don't really have a clue. They think these are just the regular fireworks I bought at some roadside stand, and out here no one's around to call the cops. I work for that one night all summer, the best night of my life. I make the fireworks in the back of the shed behind the lake, the place where we store all the lawn mowers and Weed Eaters, and no one ever goes in there but the yard guy and me.

After getting my supplies and the galleys of The Dad's new book (*Taking Up Your Cross: Beginning Weight Training for Christians*), I drive around town for a while, trying to make sure I get home after the hunters are gone. Asheville is a pretty cool place, a coffee-bar-and-movies-with-subtitles kind of place. I like it. The town where we officially live is Tenly (don't bother; it's not on the map). The camp is eight miles outside of *that*, and Tenly isn't even really a town at all. The one big deal, ever, about Tenly was on Main Street—this big oak tree had grown all around this red fire hydrant, so that half the hydrant was sticking out and the other half was in the tree, inside the folds of bark. I mean, man, call the five o'clock news. For years people would pose for pictures around the Fire Hydrant Tree, and some would take a new picture of their kids every year, to see how much they'd grown. It was big news when they cut off the water to the hydrant and put in a new one, letting the tree have the old one. Some tenth-grader did a pen-and-ink drawing of the Fire Hydrant Tree, and the drawing was put on all the letters sent out by city hall, like the reminders to mark your driveway with sticks so the snowplows wouldn't tear up your curb. Then one day the tree just swallowed up the fire hydrant. Just a weird lump, like the tree had some kind of tumor, and it was gone forever. They had a meeting to decide if there was a way to uncover the hydrant without killing the oak. Tree surgeons were consulted. Finally they had to let it be, just know that the hydrant is inside the tree, but unseen, like knowing it's in there is enough.

Half of my brain is thinking that it isn't fair for the cops to be driving a plain white van, one that looks like it belongs to a plumber, maybe, or like my van, except mine has the cartoon cross. They ought to have to pull you over with something that at least *looks* like a police car. But this plumber's van suddenly has flashing blue lights on the dashboard, and a siren, and my hands know what's going on before I do, and they start shaking.

He asks me to get out of the van, and I do. He looks less cop-like than his van—no uniform or hat or anything. Instead he's wearing a gray hoodie and jeans and these Wal-Mart–looking sneakers, like he's ready to go play some pickup ball. But he's also wearing his badge and name tag and buzz cut. And a gun. Before I can barely notice any of this, he asks for my license, so of course out comes the fake ID, feeling in my hand like it weighs nine pounds. He squints at it under the bright sun, tipping it back and forth to read it, like his eyes aren't so good. And something about his eyes makes him look like he might be Hawaiian or something, and he's more tan than anyone you ever see in the mountains, except for the people who work for the Bronzing Barn at the shopping center.

"You know your brake light is nonfunctioning, on the right-hand side?" he says.

I shake my head. "No, sir. I thought they were both functioning."

He keeps looking at my ID. "Do you have a mechanic? I don't want to know you are out riding around with an intact hazard."

"I'm pretty much the mechanic, sir. I can fix it as soon as I get back to camp."

"Camp," he says, and I can't tell if it's a question or not, but I point to the side of the van, anyway. His whole face relaxes as he sees it. When dealing with authority figures, I guess it's good to have Jesus on your team. Just as I figure I'm about off the hook, I relax enough to notice something I hadn't a minute ago, the name on his name tag: OFC. TOY.

His last name is Toy, a name I haven't heard before. And I'm sorry, but this is just how my brain works. I start to think that maybe if I get rowdy he'll have to call in Ofc. Puppet and Ofc. Bouncy Ball for backup. Then I'm picturing the whole thing, imagining that anytime Ofc. Toy goes for target practice, some giant kid has to come along and snap the plastic gun into his grip. Or that one day he will be missing a leg that's lost under the sofa.

"Do you think this is funny, Eliot?" he asks me.

"No, sir, I don't," I tell him. "I'm just nervous."

"Have you done anything wrong? Are you in violation of the law? A broken brake light is not really a citable offense, unless I'm a hard-ass." Then he points at the van again. "Sorry for the profanity."

I nod, and tell him I'm not in violation of the law. And I'm not, except for the explosives shipped across state lines to a kid using a fake ID and paying for it with stolen money. Otherwise, I'm good. And right then The Dad would be proud, because I'm praying hard, *please, God, don't let him look in the van, please don't let him run the license through the computer.* It's a pretty specific prayer, and the whole time I'm saying it, I'm picturing winning Ofc. Toy stuck inside the claw machine at the arcade in the mall.

What is wrong with me?

I want to know. Or, really, I want to know if something *is* wrong with me. If I'm normal. Why my brain runs away with me, why I'm thinking about Ofc. Toy this way even as it's about to maybe get me in some real trouble, and why I think women look like autumn, or why I can pass a good twenty minutes just standing in the grocery store aisle when I'm supposed to be picking up stuff for Sonshine Valley, and instead I've just noticed a new ice-cream flavor called Chipitty-Dough-Dah. Then I'm imagining the meeting where a bunch of men in suits and ties sat around and tried to come up with that, all the names they might have discarded along the way, and I want to know if they had fun saying Chipitty-Dough-Dah over and over, or was it just another day at the office? Does everyone think that way? I really want to know. And here is the thing . . . I don't think it matters if it's normal in general, as long as one person thinks it is, or at least thinks it's OK. If you could have that person in your life all the time, and you could show her every little oddball nugget your brain digs up, and she thought it was OK, if she thought you were smart or funny, then it would be OK. Normal or not wouldn't even matter.

Ofc. Toy decides to let me off with a verbal warning, and he blesses me for the work I do. Too shaky to drive, I pull off my hoodie and toss it in the seat and lock the doors and just walk around the sidewalks for a little bit, past the art stores and the smells of cinnamon and frying food. And right when I start to breathe again, when I feel the cool of my own sweat under the Jesus shirt, I see a girl riding by in a car, some beat-up old Datsun, and for like a nanosecond I think I know her and I start to wave. I realize as soon as my arm shoots up that I don't know her, that I don't know anybody, but I can't stop looking at her, right there not ten feet away from me, just rolling past. She has these thick spirals of red hair, eyes that shine green even through the glass of her window, and then she sees my half wave and flashes me a smile, this burst of white at the middle of all that green and red, like an explosion of white, like light, like a smile that knows exactly how perfect it is.

Like fireworks.

3 calliope

I remember hearing the squeak of the chains as Delores swung back and forth, drifting on the bench swing on the front porch, while heat from the Texas sun slowly rose off the baked earth. My father, Frank, began staying in his studio at the back of the lot late into the night. I lay awake every night, listening to the sound of his electric wheel drifting in through the windows as he threw pot after pot.

It might have been the dogs. I can't say for sure. There were just so many of them, and it probably wouldn't have seemed like as much of a big deal except that Frank let the lease on the building next door lapse. The new renters wanted the dogs out of there so that they could bring in their stuff. But there just wasn't enough room for them all. We had three in our living room alone. Frank kept telling Delores that the dogs would sell as soon as the weather got better, but they didn't. They just sat hunched around the parking lot, cement baskets meant to hold flowers clutched in their jaws. It was almost as if those dogs were cursed. Rainwater filled the baskets, becoming murky and slimy in the humid spring air. SUVs drove away with birdbaths, hedgehog boot scrapers, pavers with Hindu symbols of peace and serenity, and hand-thrown planters. One designer from Austin, working for an eccentric client, cleaned us out of every stone pineapple and monkey. Even the stone vases with feet shaped like elephants sold, but the dogs didn't. They huddled around the lot in groups of twos and threes, waiting.

Sometimes I would sit at my window, staring out into the night. The sign for Garden Arts, faded from the hot Texas sun, swung from the rusted archway, curving over our driveway. Even in the dim light of the dying moon, I could see our three handprints, mine in the middle, a crack in the baked wood neatly bisecting my palm.

Every Faire has its own slant. Some are more arts-and-crafts festivals, while others function as authentic Elizabethan towns, complete with blacksmiths, bakers, knights, royalty, and jesters. The one in Asheville seems more like the second kind. There's a hierarchy in Faires. The jousters and knights are at the top. The artisans and performers are next, showing off their talent with leather and metal and magic. Oddly enough, the royalty is next. There isn't any real skill required to walk around in a pretty dress and allow people to kiss your hand, or to tap kneeling men on the shoulders, turning them into knights for a day.

At the bottom are the service people. The brewers, the food purveyors, the stable keepers. And the wenches.

Delores is one of the few to exist on two levels. She spends all morning answering questions about her rings and necklaces, sliding bands of silver filigree on fingers, and draping ropes of gold and amber around throats. I usually take over the booth just before lunch, giving her enough time to change her clothes. She slides into her skirt and blouse, pulling them right over her shorts and tank top. I hold up a blanket in the back of our tent more for the sake of authenticity than modesty. I watch as she cinches her vest, lacing the black ribbons tightly across her chest. Her breasts, normally small and round, grow, pushing up and out and threatening to spill from the top of her blouse. The addition of a silver mug, hung from her neck on a heavy linked chain, nearly finishes the look. Delores closes her eyes and I see her pull inward, shifting herself deep inside. When she opens them, a vacant smile blooms on her face. I wonder if anyone else can see the thing she is missing. When she shifts, one thing gets left behind. When she opens her eyes, no one is home.

"Why don't you catch a ride into town?" Delores asks after we finish breakfast. I fold my napkin around the rest of my blueberry bagel and add it to the banana I have stuffed in the kangaroo pocket of my sweatshirt. "I'll probably just be doing a lot of paperwork and setup today." She looks around the tent at the clusters of Faire workers huddled at the various picnic tables.

Our jouster friend is sitting with a couple of women dressed in matching T-shirts, the words KEEP THY WITS ABOUT THEE emblazoned on their backs. Faire people are crazy for witty T-shirts. The best I have in my collection is one that says REFORMATION on the front and I DON'T BUY IT on the back. Delores has an INTERNATIONAL WENCHES GUILD shirt, but she won't wear it to Faire. We both watch Phi as the two women across from him laugh.

"I think they're lesbians," I say, lifting my cup to my mouth.

"Who?" Delores asks. I roll my eyes at her. She squints at me for a moment, deciding. "What makes you say that?" She balls her napkin so that she can shove it into the spout of her milk carton.

"I saw them kissing this morning on the trail when I went out for my run."

"Maybe they're just friends," Delores mumbles, finally succeeding in pressing the rounded paper into the triangular opening. Reality wavers for a moment as I try to figure out what she is thinking. When I don't answer immediately, Delores looks up at me. I see an unfamiliar urgency there with the flecks of gold in her pale eyes.

"I saw tongue," I say, pushing myself to standing. She shrugs as if nothing happened. She walks toward the trash can, nearly overflowing with plates and cups and banana peels. "So, I'll see you later," I say to her retreating back. She lifts her hand without turning, wiggling the backs of her fingers at me. I am dismissed, apparently. She has gotten what she needed.

* * *

I hang out near the registration tent, watching for anyone heading toward the parking lot. A man wearing a baseball cap and glasses slides past me and smiles. "He's headed into town, sugar," the woman who checked us in tells me. "Abel, honey," she calls after the retreating figure. "Can you give this young lady a ride into town?" The man stops and turns toward me. He's older than I thought, maybe thirty. Maybe forty. He cocks his head to the side, looking at me. His eyes crinkle at the corners as he smiles.

"The name's Abel. As in Cain and . . ."

"Mine is Cal. As in . . ." I can't think of anything to finish the joke, making his smile bigger.

"You're welcome to a ride," he says. "So long as you don't mind the smell." He leads the way to the parking lot. I'm not sure what he's talking about until I see the sign on the side of his pickup. THE CLOVEN HOOF. "I sell barbecue," he says, jingling his keys. "I know what you're thinking," he continues, sliding onto the bench seat. The inside of his truck smells of garlic and cayenne and some other spice I can't quite place. I roll down my window as soon as I shut my door, but not before a sneeze escapes.

"What am I thinking?" I ask, pulling my bagel from my pocket and using the napkin to blow my nose.

"You're thinking, 'What's a nice Jewish boy like me doing way up here in the mountains selling pork ribs to a bunch of kooks in tights?'" I wasn't thinking that, but I nod anyway. "Well, I figured there's really only two ways to go when you finish rabbinical training."

"Oh yeah?" I ask, turning to look toward him. An earring flashes in one ear. Onyx maybe.

"As I figure it, you can either go into a temple and never come out, or you can buy a pickup, load it full of a couple hundred heads of garlic, ten pounds of chili powder, a can of turmeric, and your sleeping bag and head south. I won the Jersey Rib Cook-off, the Great Floridian, and the Texas Sesquicentennial Classic."

"Then what?" I ask, now fully staring at him.

"I decided to settle down. I've been running the restaurant in Asheville for seven years now and been trucking my ribs out here to the Faire for the last four." Abel is quiet for a moment, steering his truck out onto the pavement. "So, what's your story?" he asks, settling back into the seat.

"My mom makes jewelry," I say, staring straight forward at the yellow stripe disappearing under the front of the truck. I feel Abel's eyes on the side of my face. "She also works as a wench," I finish firmly, as if this is all there is to tell. Neither of us says anything, winding our way through the woods. We roll into town past a used-book store and a florist offering two dozen roses for $9.99. Abel makes a hard right into the alley and slides up to the back of one of the buildings.

As if we didn't just spend the last five minutes in total silence, Abel continues. "Well, that's your mom's story then, isn't it?" he asks, shifting the truck into park. He adjusts his baseball cap and pulls on his door handle before looking at me. "Her story ain't necessarily yours, now is it, darlin'?" he asks, in what I imagine to be his best attempt at a Carolina accent. I smile at him before sliding out the door.

"Remember," he calls to me after I thank him for the ride and start walking back up the alley to the main street, "be back here by four if you need a ride back out. I got to go and set up for dinner and I can't be late." He clomps up the steps to the back door. "Trust me. There's nothing worse than a bunch of hungry jugglers and mimes. They'll beat you to death with their clubs and do it without a word." I can hear him laughing even as I turn onto the sidewalk. Despite myself, I feel a smile playing at the corners of my mouth.

I think you can get a real sense of a place from the things that get thrown away. I don't mean trash. Everyone has that and it's mostly food wrappers and bits of paper and such. It's the things that still have life in them that interest me. Sofas with most of the seat cushions still intact left at the curb, a toy dump truck with a missing wheel, a frying pan with a scratch right down the center. I can almost imagine the stories attached to those things. The party and beer spill that finally made the owners decide the couch was just too stained to clean. The search that must have taken place for the missing wheel and the tears when it wasn't found. The heated words from a wife when she realized her husband had scratched her favorite frying pan after she had repeatedly reminded him not to use metal utensils on the nonstick cookware. Maybe that's one of the reasons used-book stores interest me so much. I mean, real used stores, not the ones in a factory outlet mall filled with remainders. Pages in Time on the corner of Main and Highland has a BE BACK LATER sign in the window with a fake clock, its hands pointed to one. I have nearly an hour to kill.

I walk toward what I think is the heart of town. The streets are quiet. Apparently the rich and artsy like to sleep in. I haven't always had this attitude toward money. I mean, we have never been rich. In Texas, I guess you would say that we were firmly middle class. You know, two cars, both around five years old. A three-bedroom, two-bath house. But, over the past four years, I have developed a real attitude toward money. It works both ways. I hate that we are so poor that sometimes we have to eat rice and apples for a week because we don't have enough money to buy anything else. I hate that even when I went through my growth spurt last year and I shot up four inches in three months, I had to wear the same jeans and the girls in my school made fun of me for my floods. But, here's the thing. As much as I hate that we don't have money, I hate that I sometimes want it so bad. I hate the part of me that sees the hand-painted clogs in the store window and wants them so much. I hate that sometimes I look at Delores with her torn sweatshirt and stained jeans, and phrases like *white trash* and *low class* come to mind.

I hate that sometimes I think I would trade just about anything to live in the big stone house at the end of this block. The one with the rose garden in back and the detached garage with the separate apartment over it.

Delores says that money doesn't matter and in a way she's right, but sometimes it might be nice to not have to worry all the time about everything. I mean, I think it might be nice to just be warm in the winter and not worry about how much firewood we are using. Or just buy a new coat and not have to wait until it goes on clearance sale just before summer when the only thing that's left is ugly and beige and has been tried on and trampled until it barely looks like a coat. Sometimes it might be nice just to relax, to let go of all of the voices reminding and admonishing and warning. Sometimes I just wish that there were something I could hold on to, sink into, rest on. Something that wouldn't shift away if I got too heavy. Something solid and soft and warm. Something just mine.

I take a lap around the square peering into store windows. A shop called Flights of Fancy blossoms with whirligigs, seasonal flags, box kites, and huge dragons, all rustling in the breeze. I stand, watching, as the candy maker at Sweet Endings spreads chocolate across a marble slab, working the glossy mass as it cools. He smiles at me and points to the sign in the window— FREE SAMPLES—but I shake my head and hold up the last nub of my banana. I check my watch and realize that it's after one o'clock. I drop my banana peel into the bin, walk back up the street, and let my fingers glide through the silky threads of the kites as I walk past.

I slide a book from the shelf, pulling at the top of its spine. In third grade we had to watch a film called *A Book's Life* before we were given our library cards. Along with other rules, I remember the monotone voice admonishing us not to pull books from shelves this way while a cartoon book with a bandage wrapped around his spine/head writhed in pain on the screen. The problem is, when books are crammed in like this, pressing against one another while others push from above, I'm not sure how else you are supposed to get them off the shelf. I flip it open to the first page. I have a system. Read the first page, flip to the middle, finding a page with a lot of dialogue, and then read the first few sentences on the jacket or the back of the book.

"You won't like it," a voice says. I turn my head to the left. He's not looking at me but down at the book in his hands. I look beyond him, but there isn't anyone else in the store. He turns to face me, and I am startled by two things. First, his eyes are the darkest blue I have ever seen. Almost black. Second— and this is the thing that makes me keep looking much longer than I normally would—his lips are green. I mean really green, like if suddenly the lights went out in the store and the sun went black, I could probably read by the light his lips put off. I keep looking at him, waiting for him to say something else. There's a voice in my brain that is screaming at me and getting louder. *Say something,* it tells me. *Converse,* but all I am thinking is *Blue Green, Blue Green, Blue Green* like some sort of moron, and the best I can come up with is "Why?" And in my brain I'm thinking, *Why do you keep looking at me that way? Why won't I like this book? Why are your lips green? Why are you talking to me?*

"I have some rules about books," he says, and my brain goes into overdrive, echoing everything he says like something messed up the audio in a movie and instead of one guy with green lips talking to me, there's two. The one in front of the science section in the bookstore and the one in my brain. And the one in my brain is talking to me like I am an idiot. *He has some rules about books!* the brain guy says to me, like I wasn't listening or was too dumb to understand English.

Luckily my brain still seems connected to my mouth because I hear myself say, "Oh yeah?" in what I hope is a slightly sarcastic but not too caustic way.

He turns to face me and suddenly I am aware that he's tall, really tall, and along with the crazy voice in my head still echoing the last sentence he said and the percussion section stomping out *Blue Green, Blue Green,* I have something else, a buzzing like a hive of bees has just erupted in my head. And I have to strain to hear what he is saying because on some level my brain is aware that it should listen.

"It's simple really. No books with neon or metallic printing on the cover. No books with three-word titles that seem constructed by some publishing rubric. *The Shattered Heart, The Raging Storm, At Full Throttle.* And especially nothing that has a cutout on the cover, so that you get like a double cover when you lift the real cover." As he talks, he keeps his eyes lowered, looking at the book in his hands, but when he finishes he looks up at me again and smiles. And all I can think is *Dear God, someone better open a window because it feels like it's a thousand degrees in here.* Apparently my brain does OK in the heat because I feel my lips working and I hear myself saying something. I listen close, wondering what it is. "So, you're saying that you judge a book by its cover."

"Yeah," he says, shifting *Chemistry for Beginners* in his hands. "But see, I mean it in a purely non-metaphorical way." And suddenly everything gets quiet and I brace myself for the noise. Sure enough it comes. The brain guy starts yelling *non-metaphorical* like he's one of those chest painters at a football game and the percussion instruments start beating out some sort of salsa rhythm for the bees to dance to. I nod when the real guy says he'll see me around. And the way he says it, I think he actually means it. And I stand there watching as he pays for his books and waves. The band keeps rocking in my head, but as I listen I realize that there is something else there, real soft underneath the crashing. I can't quite identify it, but it's there— a sustained note. It's something quiet and peaceful, and all I can do is smile and lift my hand because my brain is too busy throwing a party in my head to think of anything clever to say.

✳ ✳ ✳

"Can you give me a hand?" Abel asks, spotting me sitting on the back steps. I put down the book I'm reading. No neon, no metallic, no cutouts, and four words in the title. I head into the kitchen and help him haul steamer trays full of ribs and plastic tubs of sauce out to his truck. Once we have loaded the corn bread, coleslaw, and cobbler, he offers me some tea. "Regular or unsweetened?" he asks.

We sit on the back steps, in silence for a few moments, feeling the sunshine and sipping at our glasses. His sweet, mine not. "So what's gotten into you today?" he asks. I look at him and shrug, not quite trusting myself to speak. He watches me as I struggle to keep my face neutral, failing miserably. "Hmmm," he says, "Someone's got a secret." He stands and brushes off the back of his jeans. As I follow him to the truck to head back to the Faire, I can't help thinking that he's right. Exactly right. I do have a secret and the voices in my head invent a bouncing melody with the words. And I find myself humming along as the brain guy does a good impression of a jazz crooner with a whole mess of bees for backup singers.

I have rules for things, like which apples are edible (snaps when you bite it, crunchy, no grit, ice-cold), or how to choose a book from a bookstore, or how to lie (like I said before), or how to make a bed (I make a lot of them at the camp), or how to make coffee (put the cream in first, and you don't need to stir it). When you grow up the way I do, and the biggest thing in your life so far has been getting dunked in a glass tank by a man who acts like he's mugging you but says instead he's saving your soul, then celebrating your soul mugging at Sizzler with your parents (get the buffet by itself, not added on to a steak dinner, because the buffet already has sirloin tips), you need rules. And not their rules, not God's rules, but mine. My own. Here's one of Eliot's Rules for Dating:

> *When you first meet a girl, make sure you are*
> *accidentally conducting a chemistry experiment on your lips.*

OK, I didn't say they were all good rules.

As much as I can figure out, in the last thirty-six hours, here's what happened. After I got the load of chemicals back to Son-shine Valley, I went as fast as I could to stash them in the stor-age shed, and then I opened up all the plastic tubs (the kind they sell cheapo ice cream in) and took out the plastic bags to make sure my order was right, and just then I heard Peto com-ing in, hanging the Weed Eater up on the wall, dipping into the bag of corn to bait the geese for the hunters. So of course he knew I was there because the van was parked outside, and so I just shoved everything, the tubs and the plastic bags, back up under the workbench and pulled the paint tarp down to cover it all. Yeah, I know, real sophisticated system I have. So anyway, I talked to Peto for a while and he offered me a dip of Skoal like he always does and like always I said no, and already through the open door I could see the hunters pulling up, getting out of their cars in their little camo suits, and then Peto went out to talk to them, and I had to get out of there.

Next morning I went back in to straighten everything out, on my way into town again. You may not know this, but almost all the chemicals are white powder with no smell. I mean, I could've had ten bags of baking soda sitting around in there, and I had to get the bags back into the right buckets, like it was some kind of party game, and the only way I know how to do it is by taste. I know, I know . . . I mean, in ten years this stuff is probably going to make me grow a tumor or a second head or something, but I didn't know any way else to do it. It's like detectives on TV, when they taste the stuff in the Baggie and then say, "Yeah, that's pure white lady—book him." I'm pretty sure that doesn't happen since they have labs and scientists, but I don't, so I had to taste it. Potassium chloride tastes like cotton candy and hair spray, while sodium chloride tastes like milk gone bad. It's pretty easy.

Here's the weird part. I'm almost sure the green must have come from the potassium chloride, but it can only turn green in the presence of alcohol. No, I don't drink, I never have. The irony here is that I was headed to the bookstore in town to find a book on chemistry, because the better chemist you are, the better pyrotechnician you are. Anyway, here's my theory:

Gum.

In fact, it was Dentyne Ice Peppermint, which like all gum contains sorbitol, which is an alcohol sugar. So I went into town with potassium chloride on my mouth, just a dusting of it, then see this beautiful girl, and I know I want to try to think of something to say to her, and so I pop a piece of gum in my mouth just like the guys on the commercials, only they never show on the commercial the guy ending up like he's decorated his lips for St. Patrick's Day. Never. That would just be me.

And it wasn't just some girl, it was her. *Her.* When I tell myself the story for the eight hundredth time so I can kick my own butt for the eight hundredth time, that's about all the explanation I need: *her.* In the bookstore, I said it over and over to myself . . .

it's her, it's her, it's her. Fireworks girl, the one I'd just seen the day before and started to wave at like I'd known her all my life, and the more I looked at her there in the musty stacks, the more I thought I *had* known her all my life. I mean, I probably looked creepy, I was probably staring, and staring is worse, I'm sure, if you're running around with green lips, but of course I didn't know that. All I knew was that I couldn't really breathe, and that her hair was as thick and red as any I'd ever seen, and that her eyes looked smart as she scanned the books, like there was so much going on in there, lots of complex machinery, but machinery made of flesh and blood. She looked like she believed in something, or wanted to, and I hoped to hell it wasn't God, not in the way The Dad believes, because all that does is make him forced and desperate. No, it was something else, not just that I saw a pretty girl and just got all excited. I mean, yeah, that part is true, and she really was gorgeous, and the freckles covering her, the freckles on top of freckles all spread out and folding into one another made her skin look like it had grain and texture, like polished wood, like it would feel smooth to the touch, and so soft. I knew that. But it wasn't how she looked. You could walk down the sidewalk any day of the week in Asheville and see hundreds of beautiful girls, all different types and ages and all different hair and clothes, so it wasn't that. It was something else.

What? I don't know, exactly. She seemed to be inside something, inside herself, as if all that beauty had been made in her as this big hall full of chandeliers and marble fireplaces—beautiful but empty. And she'd been dropped down in the middle of it and had spent too many years wandering around in it, her footsteps just echoing inside herself, wondering if anyone else was there, wondering how she'd got there, telling herself that if she had to be alone in there, at least she had interesting things to look at. Only she didn't want to be alone in there, and since she was never going to find her way out, someone would have to find his way in. I knew all of that, and it took about ten seconds to figure it out. And it took another ten to figure out that I wanted to be the one to push open those heavy doors and wander those empty halls calling her name until I found her. But how do you do that when you aren't really in a great hall but only a bookstore, and you don't even know her name, and your gum has made your lips turn green?

I tried, and I talked to her, I told her my rules for choosing a book. I was cool, at least I thought as much until I got into the van and saw my mouth in the rearview, but it's not enough, is it? I'm just some guy who spoke to her in a bookstore, and if you look like her I'm sure there are guys speaking to you all the time—she probably has guys coming up to speak to her when she's in the middle of the car wash. A good number of them likely have normal-looking lips. So where does that leave me?

It leaves me where I'm always left. At the camp, the mountains around us like a well, and me trapped at the bottom. All day long I have been at it, because the first fat campers arrive soon, and everything has to be ready. I've been making beds and sweeping floors and changing AC filters and raking the exercise trail and hauling bottled water into the cafeteria. And I get all my usual jobs done twice as fast so I have time left over to make fireworks. I want something to happen. Maybe that's all fireworks are: you make something happen. I pick up a Spangle shell I've been working on. It's not rolled tightly enough, but it will do. But I need to get better at it, better at fireworks. If I'd paid more attention in the poetry part of English class last year, maybe I could say something about how the shell is like my chance with her yesterday in the bookstore, how a fuse gets ignited somewhere inside, and all you want to do is watch it climb out of dark and explode into something beautiful. But the truth is I don't know much about poetry, and all the poems we study at Lighthouse Academy are about Jesus and not one by any poet you ever heard of, and half the fireworks I make end up as duds because I'm not any good, and the fuse goes out. That's pretty much what yesterday feels like.

I'm thinking all of this when I hear the car doors slam and I walk out of the shed. There at the main building beside the lake are two cars and a pickup truck, and like it's circus-clown cars, about ten hunters come pouring out of the doors, wearing their camo and carrying their guns. The Dad and Mom are way over up at the other lake, getting the paddleboats in the water, so I walk out.

"I'm sorry," I tell the first guy. "The goose massacre was yesterday."

He takes off his Carolina Panthers hat to rub his gray hair. He looks like that guy on TV who sells supplemental life insurance. "Well, naw," he says. "We got invited back an extra day, on account of so many."

"So many hunters?"

"So many geese. Got a two-day permit."

"Well," I say to him, "maybe you could leave us with *one* goose. You know, just a token goose, so we can still say we have a goose pond."

He smiles. "You can have all that attitude, son. We don't harvest some of these birds, you'll have a worser problem, lots of disease, not a clean place to walk."

That fast, I don't like this guy.

"'Harvest,'" I say. "I think you mean 'kill.' I don't remember planting geese this year, just the tomatoes."

"Like I said, you can have it." And without another word he racks and raises his gun and fires into the geese that sit on the bank of the lake in gray and white and black clusters. And one of them explodes, all feathers and blood.

I grab the barrel of his gun and it's so hot I have to let go. "God, how about a little warning next time?" I say to him.

"Your daddy wouldn't like you taking the Lord's name in vain." He smiles and winks at someone behind me. "Next time I'll do 'Ready, Set, Go.' Okay, son?"

"Man, you jumped out of your frigging skin," the person behind me says. He's sitting on the hood of his car, smiling, gun crooked in his arm. A little diamond flashes in his right ear.

"Oh, hey, I didn't see you," I say to him. "That camo shirt is *really* effective." Yeah, trying to be cool, trying to be funny, but I can hear my own voice shaking. The flock of geese that took off when the first shot was fired do nothing more than circle once around the lake and then skitter down to the water. Then ten or fifteen guns start firing, the hunters barely out of their cars, and the smoke burns my nostrils and the sound threatens to deafen me. I crouch down, shrinking away from it and trying not to look, but I can't help it. The heads of several geese just vanish, and then their bodies tip and roll down the bank into the shallow muddy water, and the water grows dark red, like wine, in a slow-spreading pool, and I'm shouting for my mom, but of course no one can hear me, and I'm wishing I wasn't such a wuss about this, I mean, half the guys in my class hunt, but I don't like it and I never have. The geese make crying sounds, panicked sounds—like a pack of noisy kids—and they keep leaving and coming back, circling around, flying back into their own demise, unable to leave the place that's going to kill them. I hate it, hate it all, wish for a second they were just shooting one another so it would quit, and I hate this place and the mountains and the camp, hate the fat campers and Mom and The Dad for bringing me here, hate myself for my green lips and all the ways I wish I could be and aren't. I squat down behind a car, hands over my ears, and all I can think is that if I had gotten her name, if I just knew that, just her first name, I could close my eyes and say it over and over again until the shooting stopped, and it would be something to hang on to.

The next morning, a miracle happens.

I'm half asleep and the window is open in my room of the cabin, a cicada buzzing against the rusty screen. I'm trying to push myself awake, but I was up late last night, after the hunters left, in the shed making a new Spangle shell I haven't named yet. I made that one because it made me think of her . . . it's red and green and white. It's already hot out by nine in the morning, and I kick all the sheets off, and that's when I hear the car pull up. The first thing I think is that the hunters are back, and the whole scene's in my head again in an instant, and I see them leaving, carrying the birds upside down by their black legs, the necks swaying and staining their camo pants. I close my eyes. God. Maybe they are coming every day now, part of the routine. The paperboy, then the mailman, then the hunters there to kill thirty geese in ten minutes.

But I hear only one car, and then I hear The Dad using his bookstore and TV voice, asking if he can help them, and then a woman's voice, and it sounds loud, but not confident-loud really, kinda more like unsure-loud. I kneel on the bed and look out through the narrow window, and there she is—bookstore girl, fireworks girl, all the names I have for her that aren't her, standing next to The Dad and some other woman. This is so much like a dream that I figure any second that Abraham

Lincoln is going to fly above their heads and then, I don't know, a whale will swallow them all, but this is no dream. It's *her*. My heart struggles to remember what beating used to be like, and I look away. I look at my pillow, all lumpy and bunched up, but it's not really offering any explanations.

In two seconds I'm pulling jeans up over my boxers and a T-shirt over my head and I'm out the door and pausing on the porch to yawn and stretch, like I have a script that says, *pause on porch, yawn, and stretch*. Then I act like I've just seen them, and then I act like I'm just wandering over to see if I can help out, because, you know, I'm just generally helpful that way.

"Hi," I say, and trying to play it off, I stupidly say it to The Dad.

"Well, hi, son," he says.

"Like I was saying," the woman says, her necklace sparkling in the sun, "we can pay, and we don't make much noise."

Fireworks girl looks at me. "Your lips aren't green," she says.

I can feel The Dad staring at me, and I know I'll have to explain somehow later. I'll just tell him it's the latest teen slang, and he's so clueless, he'll start using it next week. I'll walk in to breakfast, and he'll say, "Hey, sport! Your lips aren't green!" and I'll have to laugh and say his aren't either. This could last for years.

"Well, not yet," I tell her. "But it's only morning."

She laughs, flashes those perfect teeth, and I imagine I can feel the soles of my feet melting into the gravel.

"Eliot?" The Dad says. "Why don't you show Calliope around while I talk business with her mother."

I nod and we start off and I pretend the gravel isn't killing my feet.

"Eliot, huh?" she says. The thin fabric of her long T-shirt brushes my arm. "Is everyone in your family named for a famous symbolist poet?"

"No, I'm named for someone who was supposed to be in the Bible but isn't."

"No? What happened to him?"

I glance over at her, the way the corner of her mouth turns up, half-smirk, half-smile. Her hair moves as she walks.

"He was called to be a disciple, but he had, you know, stuff to do."

"Stuff, like . . . polishing his sandals? Making lunch?"

We keep walking, over the bridge across the lake, past the swings and the playground equipment, just walking.

"Exactly. And what about you, Calliope . . . is everyone in your family named after a . . . what is it? A keyboard? An organ?"

"It's a steam-powered piano. It's also the name of the Greek goddess of poetry. You should read stuff other than chemistry; you'd know these things." Her smirky smile again, her sleeve touching my arm.

I feel like my skin has been removed, every nerve exposed. I open my mouth, and this comes out: "I think you are more goddess than piano." Stupid, *stupid*.

But she laughs. "You know, that's the nicest thing anyone's said to me today."

"You don't see too many calliopes," I tell her.

"I'm Cal, actually. I mean, that's what I prefer."

"I meant the steam pianos . . . you don't see too many." She stops and looks at me, full-on, and right away I put it on the list of the best moments in my life.

"Until you said that, Eliot, I wasn't fully aware of the demise of the steam piano, so thank you. Really."

I smirk at her and we both fight not to smile. "Okay, smartass," I say.

"Wait, you're the God Guy. You can't say that." Her green eyes, I see in the sunlight, are flecked with gold, like tiny nuggets in the bed of some mossy stream.

"I'm just son of God Guy," I say. "Don't hold it against me."

"I promise I won't. So, tell me something."

We stop again, beside the old mini-golf course, which is all grown over with weeds. I notice some kind of necklace—a bottle cap on a string, really—hanging around her neck, and so she doesn't think I'm just looking at her breasts, I say something about it.

"What is that?" I ask her.

She looks at me for half a beat. "It's a bottle cap on a string."

"I can see. I meant, why are you wearing it?"

She shakes her head, smirky again, but I see something else . . . a blush, which seems to burn deep under the layers of her freckles. "I asked you to tell me something, not me to tell you something."

"Tell you what?"

She is looking at me now, leaning against the rotted remains of the building where you used to get putters and the little colored balls.

"Tell me *something*. Some people collect stamps. I collect stuff people tell me. It's easy to take with me when I move away."

The idea of her moving away feels like a spike hammered deep in my gut, but I try to concentrate on something to tell her. "Well," I say, "speaking of pianos, Thomas Edison once invented a piano made of concrete. Not up there with the light-bulb, is it?"

She scrunches up her nose, shakes her head, hair spilling over her shoulder. "Nah, that's like a *Jeopardy!* answer. I want you to *tell* me something."

"Okay," I say. Don't ask me why, don't ask me what I saw in her to trust with everything. I don't ask myself that as I hear myself speak: "I make fireworks, illegally, with chemicals that I order, illegally, with a fake ID, using money stolen from my parents. And I shoot them off, and they are beautiful. . . ." I linger over that last word, my gaze caught in her eyes, in her face, in her hair. "I'd like to show you that sometime," I say. "I'd like to show you everything."

5 calliope

I woke up this morning and had the same wish that I have had for the last seven mornings. It seems like a simple one. I wish that we could live somewhere with a real floor and a door and a kitchen (don't get me started on kitchens), somewhere that has windows without zippers. I mean, I still had that wish, but there was another wish crowding that one, so that the house wish had to scrunch up a bit and pull in its knees. The other wish was about "The Guy with the Green Lips." I kept calling him that all night in my head, like he was some kind of action figure or some B-movie character dreamed up to chase girls in twin sets and circle skirts. Only now I know his name. It's Eliot. Although I'm not sure if that's with one l or two, and for some reason that keeps tripping me up a bit even though I'm just thinking about him and not trying to write him a letter.

I woke up this morning thinking about those two things: the house and the guy, so it's weird the way those two things kind of came together. Phi told Delores that sometimes the God Guy on the hill rented cabins to people during the summer. So, I was standing there just half listening to Delores tell the God Guy that we would be good renters when The Guy with the Green Lips starts walking across the gravel toward us. The God Guy introduces him as his son and I was thinking about seven million things in that one second, but the three that I could pull out of the mess were the following:

1. If he was the God Guy's son, did that make him the Messiah?
2. Why, even with his hair sticking up and his face all kind of red where he had been sleeping on it, was he so damn cute?
3. Wasn't the gravel killing his feet?

I didn't ask any of these questions. Instead I stuck to the obvious. But right off when I asked about his lips, I knew it was a mistake because he got nervous, but it wasn't directed at me, but at his dad. So immediately I'm thinking that someone else has a secret—and for a crazy moment, I thought maybe the secret was me, but then I made myself stop thinking that because it just wasn't possible he would think that too.

I kept bumping his arm while we walked, but I can't say whether that was my fault or it was more the fact that the sharp rocks were making him walk unevenly, placing each foot carefully. We stopped by the windmill, its broken arms dangling over the weeds. I was so close to him that I could smell him, the warm sleep smell that makes me think of blankets and fireplaces and scrambled eggs late at night. I started to put my hand on his arm to see if it was as warm and solid as it seemed. Just to see how my pale fingers would look on his tanned forearm. Just to feel him. Touch him. And then he asked about the necklace.

I read somewhere that if you think you're going to cry, you can recite the colors of things to make it stop. Green tree. Red windmill. Blue sky. Blue jeans. Blue eyes. I wanted to tell him. I wanted to tell him all of it, but that was crazy, wasn't it? I mean, I just met him. So, I did what I do. I asked him to tell me something. The amazing thing was that he *did,* and when he looked at me, I felt not the rush I felt yesterday, when it seemed like the whole world was awake and alive and singing, but something else. Something big and profound and bottomless. Something that answered another question, one I wasn't even aware that I had asked. Standing there next to an overgrown mini-golf course in the middle of the woods in North Carolina, I heard an answer. And the answer was yes.

So, I'm sitting at the picnic table making a list of reasons why I shouldn't be thinking this about Eliot—or Elliot—and number one at the top of the list is this: I just met him. But for some reason that doesn't seem like enough, so I try to think of more things to put on my list, but so far all I have are the numbers lined up along the left side of the page like I have prepared my paper for a spelling test.

Delores told me that the God Guy didn't have any cabins for rent, but I couldn't tell if that was true or if she just decided that maybe the God Guy seemed too normal, too nice, too something. So, I guess it's tent city for a while longer. I get angry with her sometimes, but something stops me from saying it out loud. I want to tell her that a cabin in the woods beats a tent, like rock beats scissors. I mean, *every time,* but when I do say something, even a little thing, I can see her retreating and it's the leaving I'm most afraid of. Way more than living in a tent for the rest of the summer.

"What are you writing?" I look up and have to shade my eyes. Abel shifts so that he's blocking the sun, giving me time to fold the top of my paper over.

"Nothing. I was just thinking," I say. And he smiles at this new game that we have between us. Him asking questions and me not answering. So, I do my thing again, except this time I have a specific question. "Why ribs?" I ask. "Why not chicken or hamburgers or just about anything else?" I pull my knees up, wrapping my arms around them. "I mean, isn't eating pork against your religion?"

Abel lowers himself to the ground, leaning back against a tree, but a quarter of the way around so I can't see his face. "I guess the easy answer is that I like barbecuing, but I don't think that's really what you're asking." He slides lower against the tree and pulls his baseball cap down over his eyes. "I guess it's like what I told you yesterday. I wanted to find my own story. Not my parents' story, not the Boston story, not the Jewish story. I wasn't even interested in the right story. I just wanted to find mine."

I wait to see if he's going to continue, but he doesn't. "So have you? I mean, is this your story?" I ask, barely able to breathe, waiting for him to answer. A part of me wants to know that it is out there. That somehow, if you are patient and keep looking, one day it will happen.

He shifts lower, as if the burden of telling me is too heavy to sit up under. "Some days it feels more like a sitcom or a limerick than a story. *There once was a Jew named Abel . . . who dreamed of filling his table. With his ribs and cobbler, he made people slobber—*"

"Um, I'm not sure that *cobbler* and *slobber* rhyme," I say, smiling at him. "I'm sorry, I interrupted. Please continue."

"Well, that's all there is so far."

"No, with your *story*, not your limerick," I say, rolling my eyes.

"Let's see. I dropped out of school twice before finishing and realizing that I didn't want to be a rabbi. Drove my father nuts. I got married to a girl who I thought loved me. Drove my mother nuts. Drifted around for a while. Then, I came here. When I drove into town, I knew this was it."

"It?" I ask.

"Somehow this place seemed like home, but like a home I had never known before. Don't ask me how I knew because it doesn't make any sense. In fact it seemed so crazy to me at the time that I tried to talk myself out of it in a million ways."

I finger the uneven fold of the paper I am holding. "So, how did you know?"

"Well, there weren't any burning bushes or lights in the sky. One day I just realized that I could either accept what I knew to be true or continue to fight it." Abel sits up and looks at me. "I guess I finally just realized that I had to trust my heart." I'm not aware that I've been holding my breath, but it comes out in a rush. I fold the paper in my hands, making it smaller and smaller until I can't even make the edges meet again.

Abel stands and stretches his arms above his head. "Guess I'd better go get the grub on." He turns to walk back toward the tents where they are setting up for lunch. Before he's made it more than a couple of steps, he turns and looks back at me. "Hey. How did you make out with the cabin this morning?"

"How did you—" I begin, but he stops me by holding his hand up.

"Small town," he says, smiling.

"We didn't," I say, looking over to where our orange tent sits, crowded in on all sides by fifth wheels and motor homes. And for a second I get angry at Delores, but I can't say for sure just why.

"Well, I was thinking," he says. "I know of a place in town.

65

It isn't much. Just a one-bedroom. But it does have a nice kitchen and it's cheap. Maybe next time you're downtown, you should take a look at it."

"Where is it?" I ask.

"It's actually over a garage. Just down the street from the restaurant. You must have walked right past it when you were in town yesterday. The house is the stone one on the corner with the rose garden. . . ." He keeps talking, trying to help me locate the place in my memory, but he needn't have. I know exactly where it is. "I'll talk to your mom at lunch."

I watch Abel walk to the food tent, dodging some children tearing after a small black puppy. I settle back against the table, closing my eyes against the warmth of the sun. A mandolin strums in the distance and I can hear the laughter of children being entertained by the puppet-show rehearsal. After a few minutes I force myself to walk toward the craft area in search of Delores, but not before I drop the folded piece of paper in the trash barrel leaning against the side of the blacksmith's shop.

It was weird growing up in a family with two artists for parents. I mean, it never felt weird at the time, but looking back, I know that my childhood was decidedly not normal. Eating cold cereal for dinner every night for a week when Frank had a deadline was not normal. Doing my third-grade science-fair project on the properties of inorganic crystallization was not normal. The fact that Delores let me dye my feet blue when I was eight just because I wanted to wasn't normal. They would call it following my interests, finding my vision, listening to my muse. I would call it strange.

I've always been a bit odd. Too much in my head, I guess. Delores and Frank always said that I was finding myself, but I think the truth is I've found myself and I don't fit. I try to fit in. I tried out for the pep squad in fifth grade. Too peppy. I joined the children's theater when I was eleven. Too thespian. I tried the Girl Scouts, swim team, 4-H, Future Teachers of America, and Fellowship of Christian Athletes. I tried to convert to Judaism, become a vegan, learn to skateboard, play the violin, and speak French. For a week I wore a blindfold, just to find out what it would be like if I suddenly lost my sight. The summer after I turned twelve, I decided that I was going to read the classics. I even got a poster with the one hundred most influential books. Then, after reading only five, I panicked. What about literature from other cultures? What about poetry? Plays? Essays? I dropped it and spent the rest of the summer reading *Seventeen,* growing out my bangs, and trying to break the world record for bubble-gum chewing.

Delores tried to homeschool me for a while, but Frank told her it wasn't working out. I mean, her idea of homeschool meant a morning of macramé, painting, and finding my chi. Delores dropped me off in front of the principal's office at the public school. I started second grade wearing hemp sandals, cutoff blue-jean shorts, and one of Delores's artist smocks pulled over a T-shirt. Ms. Beck smiled at me from the front of the room, but that smile faded first from her eyes and then her mouth when she saw my blue feet.

It was nearly Halloween and the other girls in my class had already banded together in groups. At recess I sat by myself, a book open on my lap, pretending to read, but really wishing that someone would invite me to play four-square, or do penny drops on the monkey bars, or twist the long runners of grass into necklaces and bracelets that we could wear for the rest of the afternoon.

In class, I focused on the line that I was drawing around my hand. The marker was too big to fit between my fingers. The fingers that I needed to make the turkey's tail. I'd seen the man at the front of the room before. His shirt was too shiny and I could see a circle of yellow under his arm when he took the folder from Ms. Beck. She pointed toward where I sat trying to press the purple point between my ring finger and my pinkie. A hand on my shoulder and I followed him from the room, past whispers and pointed fingers. The week before he had come for Paul, who still wore a *Sesame Street* belt and smelled of urine. Paul had followed the man into the hall, pulling at the strap that kept his glasses from falling off. He hadn't come back.

One cool thing about this Renaissance Faire is that instead of tents and booths, the crafters and performers get real buildings to work in. From a distance it looks like an actual town, complete with gardens of lavender and sage, and stone streets. Delores's shop is between a toy maker and a woman who sells candied apples and fudge. I'm not sure how authentic the fudge is, seeing as how chocolate wasn't discovered until Cabeza de Vaca landed in Mexico, but seeing her refill her sample tray for what is sure to be the third time that morning, I don't think anyone minds. Delores has to share space with a glassblower—a woman named, inexplicably, B. *"Not as in buzz buzz,"* she told me when we met. "Just B."

Delores squints at me when she sees me, her magnifying glasses making her eyes appear buglike. *Fly and Bee,* I think, smiling. "You hungry?" I ask, thinking I want Abel to tell her about the apartment and not me. The truth is I was surprised that she even agreed to go out to see the cabins at all. Delores doesn't care about stuff like floors and porch swings and fireplaces. She would be happy enough living in the tent all summer. I had to push her to go. I think she was more interested in meeting the God Guy than in looking at his cabins.

She holds up a finger and I walk over to where the smiling candy maker has put out another tray of fudge. Popping the silky chocolate into my mouth, I consider the side of Delores's face as she bends over the twists of silver. I guess I collect things about people, wanting to know them, wanting to peel away the surfacy stuff that gets in the way. But Delores collects people like shiny presents she never unwraps. More interested in the glint and color and the oohs and ahs when she shows them to others. She is a storyteller at heart, but her stories all seem flat, featureless. In a few months, she'll tell the story of the God Guy and his son and she will have embellished it, made it bigger and funnier and brighter, but it will be a false light. The light will come from the story and not the people in it. Whenever she tells her stories, I look around at the people listening and wonder if anyone notices that the people who live in Delores's stories aren't lit from within, as they should be, but with a fluorescent lamp that casts a harsh light and leaves cold shadows.

The food tent seems much fuller than at breakfast. With opening day so close, nearly everyone has arrived. Children already dressed for the shows dart in between the tables, grabbing biscuits and stuffing them into their mouths before streaking off again to play games of tag with complicated rules and moving bases. Phi raises a hand in our direction as we enter the tent. I stand still for a moment, letting my eyes adjust to the dim light within, but Delores steps past me to a table filled with women sifting through a pile of clothes. I had forgotten one of the best parts of Faire days. Free stuff. Most of it's period clothing. Leather vests, embroidered tunics, handmade slippers, dresses with complicated bodices and too-long skirts. But usually there are a few things I don't mind grabbing. No money is exchanged. It's more of a loosely constructed barter system. Last year I babysat one of the queen's toddlers for a leather jacket. My first summer, I cleaned the seats in the theater between shows for a set of nesting dolls and a pair of flip-flops only one size too big.

Delores extracts an ornate vest from the pile and tries it on. She swims in it, but nods, slipping one of her smaller silver bands from her fingers and passing it across the table. The mass of belongings shifts and tilts, until I see it, partly hidden under a single orange sock. It disappears again as the pile moves. I reach under the leather satchel that has covered it, feeling its cool smooth surface as I close my fingers. It's not carved and decorated like Delores's stuff. There aren't any swirls of vines or braids of glass. There aren't any fairies or wood nymphs or angels. There's just the *E* carved on the locket. *E* for *Elizabethan* and *empty* and *endless*. *E* for *eggs* and *evenings* and *explosions*. *E* for *everything*. And *E* for *Eliot*.

"I'll trade it for that necklace," the woman with the red T-shirt tells me. My hand clutches at the bottle cap and I shake my head. "What then?" she asks. I agree to a week of helping her in the stables. I would have agreed to two or three weeks. Maybe the whole summer. The longer I hold the locket, the more I want it. I untie the cinnamon-scented string of my necklace and slip the locket over the end, lifting the string until the locket slides down the incline, clinking in place beside the bottle cap. As I retie the knot around my neck and slip it back under my shirt, I can hear Delores's laughter through the crowd. It's like the tinkling of glass, pretty and sharp. It's her look-at-me laugh and I wonder whose attention she is trying to get. She nods at Abel, smiling again, then turns toward me, but not before I see her look across the tent at the cluster of women now surrounding Phi. She slides a piece of pecan pie from a table and threads her way through the circle of women that has now surrounded Abel and walks toward me.

"Did he tell you about the apartment?" I ask between mouthfuls. Fudge and now pecan pie. Nice lunch. Delores kind of nods at me. "It sounds good," I continue, but Delores doesn't answer. She's too busy not looking at Phi. "He said we can go see it anytime," I say. Delores finally looks at me.

"I don't know, Cal," she begins, and I feel it again, a brief pulse and then it's gone. She looks away, scanning the corner of the tent again. "Want to come watch the jousting practice with me?" she asks, already walking toward the doorway. I follow her, dropping the rest of my pie in the trash.

"Can we go see the apartment after?" She quickens her pace and I have to push through the crowd to keep up. I see Phi's broad back heading up the street to the stables and I realize why she's rushing. "Please?" I ask, hating the whining tone.

"Sure," she says, waving the back of her hand at me. "Whatever." And I decide that's a yes and slow down. I keep walking toward the stables even after I have lost sight of her.

A week after Paul was pulled from class, I remember standing while Ms. Beck folded the letter and stuck it back in the envelope. She ran a piece of tape across the flap, making sure it would stay closed. She watched me, frowning, as I slid it into my library book.

I crisscrossed the road on the way home, trying to stay in the shadows of the trees, watching for cars as they sped past on their way to somewhere else. Stepping onto the porch, I dropped my backpack and reached into the chest freezer for a soda. There, hanging by their necks, was Frank's other obsession, obscure sodas. Mission Cola, Bubble Up, Sun Drop, King Cola. Beside the freezer stood a Mason jar full of folded bottle caps. I reached in and extracted an RC cola, then settled into the porch swing to wait.

Delores read the letter without comment and passed it to my father. He frowned at the paper, flipping it over as if searching for a secret code to its meaning. "It's not bad, Cal," he said, looking at me. "It just says you're creative." Delores pushed away from the table and walked hard into the kitchen. We sat and listened as she ran water into the sink, opened and closed the refrigerator, and broke a glass before shoving open the back screen door.

That night I lay in bed listening as they whispered from the back porch. Every now and then Delores's voice would get too loud and then quiet again. I imagined my father stroking her hair as they talked, whispering close to her neck, trying to soothe her.

"It says she's imaginative," Frank said. The swing squeaked and I imagined him pushing it slowly with his feet.

"It says she's odd," Delores said, sighing into the night. "They think there might be something wrong with her."

"Baby, there's nothing wrong with her. She's just quiet."

"Frank, they think she might be slow."

"Who cares what they think?" Frank asked, pushing off again, making the swing moan.

"I care," Delores said.

"Do you care because of what it means to Cal, or what it means to you?" Frank asked. I strained to hear Delores's answer, but all I heard was the sound of her boots, first on the wooden steps and then on the gravel of our driveway.

I must have fallen asleep because when I woke up it was still dark out but raining and my windows were closed. "Hi, jelly bean," my father said from the side of my bed. "I thought I'd never wake you up. Come on," he said, holding up my robe. "I have a surprise for you."

We sat on the stools at the island in the kitchen, smiling at each other in the dim glow of the stove light. Silently we ate, pressing triangles of blueberry pancakes and tufts of scrambled eggs into our mouths. He held my left hand in his right, awkwardly eating with his other hand. We never talked about the reason for that first midnight breakfast, even after Delores came home three days later. It was just something for the two of us. Something we did whenever one of us was feeling bad. Mostly it was around Delores, around her habit of taking off. But we never talked about the reason, we just did it. We had the last one four years later, just hours before Delores packed up the car, putting me in it with all of her other stuff. I could still taste the maple syrup as we pulled out of our driveway onto the highway headed north. Still feel the pressure of my father's hand on mine as we made the slow arc onto the freeway out of town.

I fold my arms across the fence railing, watching as the two horses begin picking up speed. The lances are braced against the horses' flanks, dipping up and down in the rhythm of the gallop. The sound of padded wood against metal echoes off the surrounding buildings as Phi delivers the first blow of the practice. When it's over and the two knights have dismounted, Delores drops from her place on the fence railing and I watch as she walks out to where Phi is standing. Her laughter rains over me and I see the sway of her hips as she walks. Everything seems to slow down as I watch her pick her way across the field toward Phi, his chest plate shining in the sunshine. When she reaches him, she touches his arm, folding her fingers around chain mail and muscle. As I watch, the sky tilts at a crazy angle and I grab at my necklace to keep from falling.

Things People Have Told Me

by Cal

- *A wench in Iowa told me that you could kill someone with just the things you can grow on your windowsill.*

- *A bartender in Bar Harbor told me that he once saw a man eat seventeen habanero peppers on a bet before throwing up on the bar and passing out.*

- *The produce manager at Shaw's in San Francisco told me that you could live for a week on your own body's waste products.*

- *A juggler in Athens, Georgia, told me that she lost her virginity to a boy who had two earrings, drove a jacked-up Cutlass, and played bass in a band.*

- *A security guard at the Faire in Dallas told me that he knitted afghans for homeless people, leaving them folded up beside them while they were sleeping.*

- *A lifeguard in Reno told me he had a plan for starting a chain of restaurants that played heavy-metal music and sold pasta. He planned to call them Metal Mangia.*

- *A girl in Oklahoma City told me she once threw herself down the stairs after her boyfriend broke up with her, but she only ended up breaking her wrist.*

- *A boy in St. Louis told me that he thought he was gay.*

"Can we try the boats?" Cal asks. Out here it is darker than night ever is, so far away from town, with no lights from houses or shopping centers or car lots or anything. All I can see is her silhouette edged by the outline of her curls, and a little bit of color, like a fire on a faraway hill.

"Look up there, you can see the Milky Way," I tell her.

"Snickers is better," she says.

"I meant the galaxy, smarty," I tell her.

"The Snickers galaxy? Is it new?"

I smack my forehead and she laughs at me. We are sitting on the dock, and I can just make out her white sneakers, moving up and down while she dangles the tips of her loose shoelaces into the water. A soda can bobs in the ripples and keeps hitting against the wood of the dock, *kank, kank, kank.*

She leans her head back so all her curls shift, her hair past the middle of her back.

"I see it," she says. "Really beautiful."

"It is, but it shouldn't be."

She dimples the surface of the water with the toe of her shoe. "Why shouldn't it be?"

I shrug. "Because it's just this white smear of light. It looks like an accident, like an industrial spill."

"So? What's more beautiful than a beautiful accident?" She says this, and right away it makes her quiet, and I wonder why but don't ask her. It's too soon for questions like that.

I say something else, just to fill the silence. "I always wonder how you can see the Milky Way by looking out at it, when we're *part* of the same galaxy, aren't we? I mean, it's like seeing the outside of your house while you're standing in your living room."

"This is why I prefer the moon," she says. She leans back to wrap her arms around her knees, and her shoulder bumps mine. "Not so complicated. It's just like our little friend, tagging along."

"You prefer it?"

"Yes, it's my favorite celestial body. What's yours?"

"I never really ranked them." I lean her way just slightly, just enough to feel the warmth from her.

"Man, if you are going to hang around me, you have to learn to rank stuff. Favorite meal out? Breakfast. Favorite breakfast? Eggs and fruit. Best holiday? Christmas and Halloween, in a tie. Best material for drinking water out of? Glass."

"What's the worst?"

"Plastic."

"You know what I learned in physics last year?"

"Jesus physics or regular physics?"

"Regular."

"Tell me." She leans toward me a little, her hair brushing against my arm.

"The moon is always falling toward us. It falls, gets caught in its orbit, falls, gets caught, falls, caught, all the time, constantly."

"Sounds like what people do."

"How so?"

"Listen, Dr. Brainiac, it's not all science. You need to see the moon as symbolic sometimes."

I nod. The soda can starts up its noise again, then the breeze moves over us. I look up at the moon, the almost-full moon, the kind that has one edge chipped off like someone dropped it.

"So can we?" she asks.

"Can we what?"

"Try the boats." She nudges one with her foot.

"Sure," I tell her. "Boats it is." After the Palm Bough charge I'd made turned out to be a dud, I dumped it out of the mortar pipe on the edge of the lake in the dark and secretly thanked the designers of the world for making shame impossible to see at night. I told Cal I would make another one tomorrow and had no idea what had gone wrong and I really did know how to make them and, and, and, just talking too fast, and then heard her shrug, the tin clank of her bottle cap and something else on the red string she wore. Somehow that shrug let me off the hook.

The boats bob at the dock beside us, chained up together like some work gang, colored like Easter eggs. I unhooked a blue one, scraping my thumb a little on the metal hook.

"Can we paddle out over the hole?" she asks.

"What hole?" I pull the boat around to the front of the dock, leading it like a dog by the chain. The air at night this early in the summer is still cool in the mountains, and I can feel goose bumps along my arms.

"The hole in the lake, goofy," she says. She wears her sneakers unlaced and I keep thinking she's going to trip and fall head-first into the water.

I put my foot on the front of the boat to steady it while she climbs in, and her hair falls across her shoulder and brushes my arm. Her smell is vanilla and cinnamon, but it's like a lid dropping down over another smell, musty clothes or an attic trunk, maybe, and I remember that she told me she's been sleeping in a tent for the last ten nights. When she leans to get in, the bottle cap falls down against whatever else is there and makes that sound again. And that sound becomes *her* sound, like the can in the water, like if I ever had to find her in the dark I wouldn't look for her, I would listen for her, and I would know that sound out of all the others in the world.

We settle into paddling the boat, knees up and awkward,

while I try to remember how to steer the stupid thing. Half of me is still not believing she is even here. It's only been a week since the first time, when we talked beside the mini golf, and it's not exactly easy to get in touch with her, no phone, no computer in the tent. Finally I found her by making an excuse to go into town every day and hanging around the bookstore. And one day there she was, just like that first time, my lips were the right color, and I asked her to come see fireworks, and she got a ride out here to find me.

"Okay," I say, "what are you talking about?"

Instead of answering she just takes my head—my ears, actually—in her hands and turns my head to the side and tells me to look. And there I finally see it . . . the big round moon reflected in the lake, water like dark oil around it.

"*There*. A hole."

"Oh yeah," I say. "But if it's a hole, how come the water doesn't drain away?"

"It's a white hole," she says. "Exactly like a black hole, like in space, but different too. It takes light in on one side and lets it out the other side. Water can't fall in, because water is dark."

"What about us? We're dark, so we're safe, right?" Even now, her eyes are only wet reflections aimed at me.

I hear her shake her head. "We're light inside, so we will fall right through."

"How are we light inside?"

"Very good question, Master Eliot," she says, and I imagine

her smirky smile. "We are light on the inside because we are happy right now. Aren't we?"

I nod. Then remembering she can't see it and I have no sound to me, I tell her yes, we are happy. Then we're quiet a minute, and the boat slowly drifts toward the middle of the lake.

"But where do we fall to?" I finally say. "Out the other side?" I move the tiller on the boat, trying to steer us toward the moon's reflection, while our legs slowly churn the water.

"We might. But since all our light is on the inside, all our falling is on the inside too." Her voice has grown quiet, almost a whisper, though it's the kind of night that if you were standing on the opposite shore you could hear every word. I hear every word and worry about each one. I mean, how do you know? If I were Cal and sitting in the other seat and saying those things to me, I would know they meant something real. But I'm only me, and I'm just listening, and how do I know if *she* means that? What if it's just me?

And suddenly I'm not sitting in a paddleboat in the moonlight with a beautiful girl. No, I'm a contestant on a game show that exists in my head. The game is called *Is It Me?* and everything Cal does—like when her elbow pushes against mine between the seats of the boat and she doesn't pull it away—the host shuffles his cards and asks me as part of the bonus round if this elbow against mine is on purpose, because Cal wants to touch me, or accidental, just a place to put her arm. I look nervously toward the audience, which consists of two hundred clones of me sitting in chairs, and I answer and say, *It's Cal wanting to touch me.* And for proof I move my elbow a bit, not enough to make her think I want to move my arm away, but just enough to let her know this is *me,* my elbow, and not just part of the boat. And no matter how I answer, I hear the buzzer and the host tells me, sorry, but he has some nice parting gifts, and I end up leaving with the Rice-A-Roni instead of the beautiful girl.

I've said it before: What's wrong with me? Why can't I just *be?*

As if she knows what's in my head, she nudges me with her elbow. "Did you fall in without me?" she says. "You're like a million miles away."

"No, I'm here. Just thinking."

"You think a lot," she says, and when I start to say something she tell me, "No, no . . . it's a good thing. I like that. What are you thinking about?"

"About the poem you showed me the other day," I tell her, realizing that part of me is thinking that, exactly.

"Yeah, poor, old J. Alfred," she says.

When I found her in the bookstore that day, she wanted me to see the famous symbolist poet she swears I'm named after, and so she pulled down a book called *Best-Loved Poems,* and opened it to this guy named T. S. Eliot, just one l, like me. She showed me his most famous poem, about this guy named Prufrock, which would really suck as a name, first of all, and second of all, his whole entire life sucks because he is going to this party and his whole deal is that he knows there are going to be women there, and he's freaking. And he's not freaking about talking to them, he's freaking about talking to them and being misunderstood, of making a move and then doing the whole crash-and-burn thing. Crashing to the ground in flames.

"You know the worst thing about him?" I say. "Not that he's afraid, but you can tell he always has been, always will be. His whole life."

"He would never park his boat over the hole in the lake."

"No, he would stand on the shore, wearing water wings."

She laughs. "With his pants rolled up."

"And no wading for a half hour after lunch."

"See, he's missing out. Get us over the moon, and we'll fall, Eliot. Don't you want to just fall?" She turns enough to look at me in the dark and I can feel her breath on my face, her smell all around me.

"Yes," I tell her, trying not to let my voice shake, trying to steer us toward the white hole, and like the moon always does, it keeps slipping away, not being where I want it to be, but I keep steering and paddling, and then on the plastic part of the seat I feel my little finger hook over the top of Cal's little finger, and for that minute there are no game-show questions, just those two flesh-and-blood fingers, just the smallest beat of a pulse between us. I squeeze her finger, and she squeezes back.

Falling.

I feel it, like she's the white hole, she's the light, and I can just let myself fall into her, tumbling like an astronaut whose safety cord is tied only to a voice that says, *wait, wait, wait.* My voice saying it, inside me. Wait, because yeah, the guy in space is weightless and it looks so beautiful and it is, but the guy who falls out of a plane, the guy whose parachute fails? He's weightless too. Most people don't know that, but I also learned that in physics last year, that falling people are weightless, which is why you see skydivers doing flips in the air. And they are weightless for the whole drop, up until the point that they hit the ground, and without a parachute they get their full weight back right then, on impact, times a thousand. It crushes them, and that's how falling people die, crushed by nothing more than themselves.

Falling can do that too. It's not all pretty, not all a dream.

Like The Dad, for example, like how he found Jesus. He'd built one of his pools, a big in-ground one with a slide and Jacuzzi and a tile deck. The whole nine yards, he liked to say. It was at this big house about ten miles from Carolina Beach, and they were waiting for the volunteer fire department to show up because for two hundred bucks they would come fill the pool with their pumper truck. So they are waiting and The Dad is talking to the owners, doing a walk-around, and he steps backward off the edge of the deep end, like those old commercials for iced tea except there is no water and he falls twelve feet still holding on to his clipboard and lands at the bottom on the cement. He broke five vertebrae in his back and neck and for a while they weren't sure he was going to walk again. I mean, it wasn't like a TV movie, and he didn't struggle heroically to make himself walk again. It was more like they said he wouldn't walk again, and then three days later they said, nah, he will, and he did, but I guess those three days of doubt were enough. I guess he did some heavy bartering with God, legs in exchange for total devotion. At least, until the fat money started coming in. So The Dad fell into a pool, and then he fell into God, and then he kept telling me to fall into paths of righteousness, and then he fell into the whole fat-camp thing almost by accident, fell away from making pools forever, fell into a ton of money.

And somewhere along that chain of events, Mom, I think, fell out of love with him.

I see it in the way her face slips down, like her gaze is no longer on him but is on something inside her. I see it in the ways she busts it out running every day, miles and miles on the treadmill, going nowhere, then lifting weights, and she looks great, but for who? I know all the magazines tell you to do everything for yourself, but that's not how I think it really works. I think you want to be beautiful in someone's eyes, you want to be seen. Like if I shot off fireworks and no one was there to watch them, and I closed my eyes. They *become* beautiful in being seen, and maybe you're not supposed to think of people that way, but I do. You don't have to be beautiful to be seen, you just have to be seen as beautiful, by someone, by one person. Mom lost that person when The Dad fell in love with God and then money. She fell in, fell out, and it doesn't matter anymore, because the person you had to catch you at the bottom is no longer there, is off doing other stuff, and their promise becomes a kind of lie, and lying is the worst, isn't it? The thing is, I know that The Dad has never *told* her a lie, not ever, and especially not lately, because that would be a sin, right? But how he acts, and what he says, and what he does, and who he is, they don't line up anymore, and the lie is in that not lining up, the lie is in not being what she needs but pretending that he is. No one says a word, and she sees it in every minute they have together. So do I.

Cal squeezes my finger again, keeps squeezing it. "Hey," she says, "stay here with me, don't keep going off in your head, okay?"

I squeeze her back. "I'm sorry," I tell her. "I'm here."

"What were you thinking about?"

"Nothing, really," I tell her, and she looks down at our hands, and I turn my hand over and let Cal's cool thin fingers sink into my palm, and then they move, both our hands moving, so our fingers lace up together. I grip her hand and she grips me back.

All around us is dark, just water, and I am looking around for the moon, then realize that we've done it, somehow, that for that minute we have slid the boat right over that white hole, and I tell Cal, "Stop," and so we pedal backward just once, just enough to hold the boat where it is, and we both look up.

"We're right under it," she says. "Don't move." And I imagine that the floor of the paddleboat is filling with that white light, pooling over our feet, glowing and warm and running out the sides, pale white light as thick as syrup, slipping down heavy through the dark water and shining back up through, lighting up our faces, slipping out all around us in a bright circle. I turn my wrist so that her wrist curves over mine, our arms twisting together as slowly as vines, and for that moment there is no down or up, just the falling, and it's everything I want, everything I have always wanted my whole life, her skin smooth and cool against mine, her hand squeezing mine slowly, hanging on to me. And all I want is to let go into it and for it not to be that other kind of falling, the kind that will break five vertebrae in my back and neck, or crush me under the weight of my own heart.

What if I fall, and Cal lies to me?

She leans into me, reaches across herself to hold my arm with her other hand, her cool fingers sinking into me, under my skin, and the boat drifts in the white light and we are no longer paddling it, just letting it be, breathing together in the quiet dark.

"Abel said it would be open." I have to try twice before the key will go into the lock.

"Not a good sign," Delores says from behind me. I have to close my eyes and take a deep breath to keep from responding. She's been saying that all morning. Things about signs and omens and prophecies. Like suddenly she's the oracle or something. I'm already frustrated with her because of the postcard, so this isn't helping much. I looked at it this morning after finding it marking the place in her book—the edge of a cluster of bluebonnets and half of a boot, peeking out from between the pages. She said she showed it to me already. She hadn't. The key slides into the dead bolt easily the second time and I twist the knob and push the door inward.

"It smells funny in here," Delores says, stepping around me and into the main room. I ignore her again and walk to the front of the apartment. The windows are shuttered with wooden shutters, kind of like you might see on the outside of a house, but here they are on the inside. I fold one side of the shutter back against the wall and immediately the room brightens. I fold the other back and I can see right down into the back garden. It's too early for the roses to be in bloom, but the lilac bushes are heavy with blossoms, their branches bent under the weight. The postcard was from my father, the writing mostly obscured by the two yellow forwarding stickers. One from the post office in Portland. The other from the one in Mount Desert Island. It was dated May 18 and contained a question about a birthday present I never received. *Call me when you can,* it said at the end. No exclamation points or capital letters like Delores would use. Just a quiet sentence on the back of a four-for-a-dollar postcard. Later I tried to peel the stickers back to see if anything was under them, a secret message maybe, but the card started ripping, so I had to stop.

I asked her if she had anything else that she'd forgotten to tell me about, but she shook her head. I trust this. My birthday present is lost along with countless other packages and letters that are probably still following me around. I feel like I'm rushing downstream with mail floating after me. Packages from Texas containing resin key chains with cockroaches suspended in clear plastic, grocery-store jewelry with my name in rainbow letters, watermelon Pop Rocks, and countless postcards of obscure roadside attractions all float behind me. If I ever stay put long enough, they might just catch up to me.

"It's just one bedroom?" she asks, her boots echoing in the empty space as she walks to the back of the apartment. And I want to say: *As opposed to our spacious tent,* but of course I don't.

Yesterday I hitched a ride into town with B, the glassblower. She got her hair cut at the barber's—(not a hairdresser, a barber. She has a buzz cut, a B with a buzz. Man). I walked down here to take a look at the place. It was locked up, of course, but I was able to see enough by peering into the window to know that it was perfect, exactly right. I walked down the steps and back up the street to the barbershop, but B was still waiting, reading *Field & Stream,* really reading it, which gave me the willies. So I kept going to the bookstore, telling myself that I was just shopping for something to read, but I knew that I was shopping for something else . . . a guy maybe. Like maybe something in a fifteen-year-old with dark, curly hair. Maybe something with a shy smile and intense blue eyes. I thought about walking right up to the counter and asking that. Asking the bored girl with orange bands on her braces if they had anything like that. Anything in an Eliot. But then I saw him. There he was, right where I saw him before, and he looked like he was shopping too. But like me, I don't think that he was looking at the books.

"The bathroom is tiny," Delores says. I take another deep breath. I've been bugging her for three days to come see this place and I want to be mad, but after last night even she can't get to me. I hear her trying the taps and I want to say: *Hello? Running water? And a toilet that you don't have to put your shoes on to go to? And a shower that doesn't smell like Doritos and mold?*

"At least it's a gas stove," she says. Maybe her whining has even gotten to her and she's trying to find something nice to say. But all I want to say is: *When was the last time you made anything that needed cooking?* And now I'm thinking that if I keep biting my tongue, it is going to be a bloody mess by the time we get out of here, so I say something.

"I think it's great," I say, and I hear a truck pull into the driveway. I peek out the window. It's Abel, coming to check on us, I guess.

"It could use a good cleaning," Delores says, and now I am starting to get mad. Really mad, but I hear Abel's boots on the steps and I bite my tongue again. For real this time, and I taste blood.

Abel steps into the doorway and he's backlit for a second like one of those paintings you see from the Renaissance where everyone has an ethereal glow. And of course thinking about saints and Jesus makes me think of the God Guy and then I am thinking about Eliot and then last night and . . .

"What are you grinning at?" Abel asks, and I realize I am. Probably a big goofy grin. I shrug at him and he smiles. Our game is still intact. He asks, I don't answer. "What do y'all think?" he asks, more to Delores than to me, and I am praying, *please be nice.*

"It's okay," she says, but in a way that lets us know that she doesn't really think so, but is trying to be polite. "How much is it?" she asks, and I pray again, *Please let it be cheap . . . so cheap she can't say no.*

"It's negotiable," he says.

"How's that?" she asks, narrowing her eyes at him, and I know what she's thinking and I want to say, *Stop it! This is Abel, not some shifty, scuzzy bartender.*

"All I mean is that if y'all like it, we can work it out." When he says this, he takes a step back and I know that he has seen the same thing in Delores's eyes and I get mad again, but suddenly I realize what Abel has said. *We* can work it out.

"How much?" Delores asks again.

"You have to pay for your own phone if you want one," he says.

Delores narrows her eyes at him again.

"How about if I help you out this summer?" I blurt out.

Abel smiles at me. "Can you cook?"

"Kind of. I mean, I can learn."

Abel turns to Delores again. "Does that sound fair?" I am thinking that even Delores can't argue this one, but I'm wrong.

"It's too far. I can't be hauling you here and back to the fairgrounds all the time," she says, like I am going to want her to chauffeur me around all day long.

"Cal can catch rides with me or use one of the bikes in the garage."

"Looks like you two have it all figured out," she says, but she's smiling now. Then all three of us are smiling at one another and I get a funny feeling just then. It's kind of like the one I had last night when I was holding Eliot's hand and leaning against him, looking up at the moon. Instead of the feeling that I usually have, as if at any moment I might just drift away from the ground and float right up into the sky, I feel heavy, like my feet are firmly touching the ground. And the weight feels like it's in the center of my chest, like my heart suddenly is full and overfull. And all of the sudden I feel like crying, but in a good way. In a very good way.

Opening day is always a mess. Everyone's Old English is rusty, the horses are nervous, the food gets burned, the jugglers drop things, the mimes forget and talk, the queen rips her dress, and at the end of the day almost everyone is really drunk. Mead and ale are what they say they are selling, but it's really cheap red wine spiced with cinnamon sticks and anise, and beer with dye added to it to make it look authentic. Delores can make a lot of money on the weekends. While the women are walking through the craft areas and sampling the fudge and the children are bobbing for apples and taking turns on the zip line, the men are in the beverage tent, sitting behind the velvet ropes, getting good and drunk. That and attempting to grope the wenches. It is as if their entire knowledge of Elizabethan life can be summed up in a low-cut bodice and the bottom of a beer mug.

The regular fairgoers buy their ale in those thousand-for-a-dollar plastic cups that you can buy at Costco, but the true fanatics have their own mugs. They pick a number at the beginning of the summer and that's their mug for the rest of the Faire. Numbers like 3 and 8 go to the NASCAR fans, and 23 is gone the first day to Michael Jordan fans. Lucky 7, unlucky 13, and 100 go fast too. Last summer, I witnessed a fistfight between two 49ers fans, both wanting number 16. Apparently the guy with the broken nose was a bigger Joe Montana fan than the one who had to get stitches in his lip, because the former was drinking out of that mug for the rest of the season.

From Memorial Day to Labor Day, Faire runs seven days a week. Rain or shine. The arcade with the giant slide and the petting zoo opens at ten. The Wenches Walk is usually right after lunchtime. The king appoints his knights at three. Jousters battle on the hour and the Mud People come out toward dusk. If you pay them a dollar, they'll eat mud. If you give them five, they'll throw mud at someone for you. I guess they are supposed to be the mentally ill of Elizabethan times. Village idiots is what they call themselves in their more lucid moments, but those are few. Mostly they will babble incoherently and yell for no reason at all, preferring craziness to real interaction.

After three days, things are starting to smooth out. I think I am even getting the hang of working the grills. I have gotten to where I can work both of them at once, leaving Abel free to take orders and serve the customers. I'd rather cook than talk. My *prithee*'s and *pray tell*'s always seem to come out more sarcastically than I mean them to.

"I think I know your secret," Abel says from behind me.

"It's called culinary skill," I tell him. "I think I might be a natural."

"I didn't mean your cooking secret, smarty-pants."

"What then?" I ask, pushing my hair out of my eyes with the back of my wrist. "My secret for bouncy hair? Creative witticisms? Fashion?" At this I perform a model turn complete with a spatula twirl. Abel grins at me and shakes his head. Mid-twirl I see what he's referring to. Standing at the front of the line is Eliot, two dollars held in his hand and a huge smile on his face.

"What I meant was that I think you have a customer," Abel says, relieving me of my spatula and thrusting a plate of ribs in my hand. "Why don't you give him these and then maybe sit with him while he eats? Make the customers happy."

I untie my apron with my free hand and pull it over my head, but when I look back Eliot isn't there anymore. "I told him to meet you at the picnic tables," Abel calls over his shoulder. "Maybe wipe that black smudge off your cheek on the way." I can hear him laughing even after I leave the food tent and start walking toward the tables set up in clusters under the pine trees.

Eliot is sitting with his back to me, watching two boys try to knock each other off raised platforms with weapons that resemble giant Q-tips.

"I think these are yours," I say, placing the ribs in front of him and walking around to the other side of the table.

He looks up at me and I see myself doubled in the reflection of his sunglasses. "Hope I didn't get you in trouble," he says, taking one of the napkins that I brought and laying it on his leg. "Was your dad mad?" he asks.

"Who? Why would he . . ." Then I stop. My *dad*, I think. How would Eliot know . . . ? Then I realize—Abel.

"I'm sorry. I just assumed," Eliot starts, and he looks away to where the one of the boys has succeeded in knocking the other off his perch and celebrates by launching his Q-tip into the air and trying to catch it.

"That's Abel," I say. "He's just a friend." Eliot looks back toward me and takes his sunglasses off. I am once again caught in the breathless feeling of looking at his eyes, but there's something else besides blue in there. I can see a sadness in his eyes as he looks at me. And suddenly I am overwhelmed by wanting to know that sadness and make it go away and make it OK. But of course I can't say any of those things, sitting at a picnic table with a plate of ribs between us, watching boys beat one another up with oversize toiletry items so I say: "Try the ribs. They're good." And he does.

"They are good," he says, around a bite of ribs. "The sauce is amazing. And this is coming from someone who knows barbecue sauce."

"How's that?" I ask.

"Well, I had a sauce recipe in my dad's first book. My own concoction."

"Really?" I tilt my head at him.

"I kid you not. 'John the Baptist Barbecue Sauce.' Something in there about anointing your chicken and ribs."

"How . . ." I start to ask.

"Middle school home ec."

"Did you wear an apron?" I ask, stifling a giggle at the thought of him in a frilly pink apron, complete with a bow in the back.

"Well, of course, but I assure you, it was a very manly apron."

"What made you take home ec? I kind of hate myself for saying this, but I thought generally only girls took that."

"At my school everyone had to take it. Our principal made all the boys take home ec and all the girls take auto shop. She told us in assembly that we were the new generation of men and women, and that she wanted all men to be able to bake cakes and all the women to change their own oil."

"Did it work?" I ask, shifting my leg so that my calf touches his. He closes the gap between his legs, trapping mine between his.

"Well, I can bake a cake," he says, shrugging at me and grinning. "I can make a white chocolate walnut cake that might just make you fall in love with me." He gives my leg a squeeze with his.

"You sure about that?" I ask, trying for nonchalance, but my voice gives me away, coming out deeper than I planned.

"I'm thinking maybe," he says, sliding his hand up onto the

top of the table. I weave my fingers into his, listening to the sounds of the breeze in the trees above us and the high-pitched laughter of the children from the arcade.

"Are you done?" I ask, pointing to the plate of ribs, still mostly uneaten.

"Are you?" he asks. "Do you need to get back to work?"

"I want to show you something," I say.

"What?" He dabs at his lips with the napkin, and for a moment I'm wishing so hard that I am that napkin that I can almost feel myself changing, becoming thin and papery and white. "Cal?" I sit back and feel myself blushing, feel it from the tips of my toes all the way to the heat at the backs of my ears. "What did you want to show me?" he asks, sliding his sunglasses back over his eyes, making me look at my own sheepish face.

"Come with me," I say, pushing myself to a stand. I start walking toward the arcade, hoping that he is following, and for a moment I am unsure. Then I feel his hand brush against mine and suddenly we're holding hands. Forget writing and tying my shoes and flipping ribs and pulling my hair back in a ponytail. Forget all of the things that I thought my hands were for before. It's almost like after today if I look at my hand, I am going to wonder why it looks so bare, so empty.

"I'm sorry about the question about your dad," Eliot says, giving my hand a squeeze.

"It was just a mistake," I say. "Not a big deal." He gets quiet for a moment and we walk along in silence, stepping carefully between the ruts left by the storage carts and the steaming piles left by the horses.

"Can I ask you something?" Eliot finally continues, and I almost answer in a smart-ass way, telling him that it's a loaded question, but I stop myself and just nod. Then I realize he isn't looking at me, so I say yes, quietly. He doesn't say anything for a few more steps so I continue.

"Eliot, you can ask me anything," I say, and I slow down so he has to look at me, which he does. But then he looks away.

"I guess it's not really a question. Not really," he says, and I nod at him again and this time he looks at me while I do it so I don't have to say anything. "I guess I just want us to always, well, for however long we know each other, to be honest with each other." And I find myself nodding even before he finishes because that is exactly what I want too. "I mean, I just don't want there to be a lot of secrets between us," he finishes. He tries to pull his hand away from me at that moment, but I don't let him, not until I say what I need to say. We stop walking.

"Please don't," I say, holding his hand tighter. "If you think you've said too much. That I'm going to think it's too much. Don't. Because maybe it would be, to someone else. Maybe if I were another girl and you were saying this to her, maybe it would seem like too much. Like maybe I don't know you well enough to be talking about things like this. But, with me, it feels right." I loosen my fingers so he can pull his hand away if he wants to, but he doesn't.

"It does, doesn't it?" he asks, looking at me, but he still has his sunglasses on, so all I can see are the twin me's looking earnestly back at me. And, then the twin me's nod and smile.

"So, tell me, Eliot, no secrets, right?" He nods at me, but with some hesitation. "What's in that barbecue sauce of yours?"

He smiles. "Well, the usual stuff: tomatoes, honey, red pepper, but it's the secret ingredient that makes it a winner."

"What's the secret ingredient?"

"If I told you, I'd have—"

"—to kill me," I finish.

"Well, that isn't allowed. You know, *Thou shalt not kill*? I would just have to be very firm with you." He starts walking again the way we'd been headed. "Where are we going?"

"Up there," I say, pointing to the top of the speed slide. We walk to the bottom of the slide and pick our remnants of rugs that will serve as our sleds for the downhill ride. I pick blue, my new favorite color. He picks orange and smiles at me.

At the top, he slides the front of his carpet scrap under the back of mine so we can ride down together. "Hold on," I say, reaching forward to grab the edges of the slide and pull us off the starting platform.

"I am," he says, and he is, wrapping his arms around my waist and pressing his cheek into the back of my neck. I start to pull us forward and send us down the incline into the pit of sponge blocks below. "Wait," he says, and I pause mid-pull, slowing our speed.

"What?" I ask, turning my head so that I can look at him out of the corner of my eye.

"It's grape jelly," he says, pressing into me. "Cheap, dollar-fifty-for-thirty-two-ounces grape jelly."

And I can't stop smiling, at the jelly, at the sun, at the sound of horses' hooves, at the drunken cheers in the distance, but mostly at the boy pressed up against my back, arms wrapped around me, holding me tight as we build up speed and begin our fall.

These aren't any ordinary sunglasses.

First of all, they're mirrored, like the kind sheriffs always wear in movies. No one can see my eyes when I wear them, and sometimes that's exactly what you want. I only wore them with Cal to look cool, but when we're talking I know I don't have to look anything, really. I just have to look like me. After someone has seen you with green lips, it's kinda hard to pull off looking cool. But the thing about these glasses is, they put some of the mirror stuff on the *inside* of the lenses, at the corners, so when you have them on and you look down and a little to the side, you can see everything behind you. Like little rearview mirrors, on both sides. I ordered them from TV, and on the infomercial it shows a guy wearing them, and when he walks past a group of girls and the girls start whispering and pointing, he sees this going on behind him and knows the girls are into him, and so he turns around to talk to them. Yeah, I'm sure that happens all the time.

I just like them because I like to see where I've been. I read once some philosopher or something, and he said that when you put a cat in a box and close the lid, how can you tell that the cat still exists? You can't, because you don't have evidence; you just have faith. Of course, I think "cat" was a stupid example because you could still hear it moving around in there, or you could smell it. If I had been that philosopher, I would have said, "If you put a spoon in a box . . ." but I guess a spoon isn't as exciting. Anyway, I think about that all the time, not with hidden stuff, but with the past, what you just left behind. Like me. I used to have this life where I walked along Carolina Beach every afternoon finding sharks' teeth, and I was learning to surf and even bought my own long board. I went to a regular school and every Friday night Mom and The Dad would rent a movie and have wine out of a box and big bowls of popcorn, which The Dad said was the feast of kings, if kings came from North Carolina, and they would send me up to bed and I would hear them downstairs laughing and happy. The next day would be hot and maybe if it was a Saturday we would wade into the surf and take home a few flounder or spots for dinner. That was my life. And now it's all gone. Everything I just listed, and maybe a thousand more things. Like the spoon in the box . . . how do I know it even existed?

So I keep my eye on things, just so they don't slip away. That's why the sunglasses. And yeah, I use them in the way they show on TV, like once at school this guy Tommy flips me the finger right after I've walked past, and I see him in my glasses, and I say, "Obscene gestures are a giant no-no around here, Tommy. I could have you sent to hell for that," and everyone must be thinking I'm psychic or something. That was pretty cool.

I used them the other way just yesterday. Cal gave me some of the ribs she cooked, and I totally screwed up and thought that guy was her dad, and right away you could see I hit the wrong button. I think I'm pretty good at wrong buttons, and I swear if I blow this one I will never forgive myself. But Cal takes me over to the slide, and we climb way up high on top of it, and I'm feel like I'm sitting on top of one of the pyramids and the whole world is below me, below us. We sit on the carpet things and I have my legs around front, and Cal puts her hands on my calves and I thought I would die, right there, I thought my legs would never work again, unless she touched them again. She could break me or heal me, with one touch of her hands. I told her about using grape jelly in my sauce, and then she scooted forward, then leaned back toward me.

"Eliot?"

"Yes?" Below us, somewhere, I heard the thump of horses' hooves.

"Look down. Are you scared?"

"No," I said. "Remember, one of us has a manly apron, and I don't think it's you."

"But are you, you know, scared?"

"No, I'm fine."

"No, really, are you scared?"

"NO!" I said, by this time laughing, my hands around her, gathering in her warmth, the smoothness of her skin, laughing into her hair, into the back of her neck hidden under all those curls. And then we started down, the wind pushing her hair back almost like a curtain around me, my face pressed into her neck. And I wanted to stay right there, for that slide to be a million miles long, for it to take twenty years to ride, and that somehow a whole life could pass by that way, my arms around her, her vanilla and cinnamon and hair all around me, her hands in mine, but almost as soon as we started we hit the bottom and stopped. We stood up and I said, "Again," but Cal had to get back to work cooking ribs. And so I squeezed her hand a final time, put on my glasses, and told her that I would make her some of my barbecue sauce sometime, all cool, and I turned and walked off into the Faire. And the whole time I saw her in the little mirrors at the corners of my eyes, watched her walk back the other way, her hair bouncing, her hips moving, and all I could think was, *Please don't disappear.*

After three days, there is no word of Cal. Of course, any word is hard to come by, because she's in this new apartment, which you'd think was the White House or something the way she talks about it, but in ways is not much better than the tent . . .

still no phone, no computer. I told her maybe we could work out some system of smoke signals or carrier pigeons. All morning I have been going crazy, making beds, cleaning cobwebs out of corners, defrosting freezers, oiling door hinges, cleaning toilets, all just to keep my mind off of her, and none of it works. All of it's mindless, so my brain just kinda says, *Hey, nice try. Now I will think about Cal while you clean that toilet.* It's hopeless. Maybe real distraction would have to be working an atomic-submarine navigation system, or computing pi to the thousandth place. Maybe that would fill up my head. Maybe.

Or maybe a drive into town.

There has to be some reason. I mean, tomorrow is the First Day of the Rest of Your Life, otherwise known as Fat Camp Day One. They arrive, all of them, on a bus from Asheville, carrying Bibles and contraband snack cakes. The big day. The problem is that just yesterday The Dad sent me into town for everything, by which I mean *everything*. He has me buy these plastic pocket combs, in case any of the boys forget theirs. I don't have the heart to tell him that boys pretty much permanently forgot pocket combs in, like, 1978. And Mom is hardly talking to anyone, just busying herself with repairs, up on the roof, under the crawl spaces of the cabins, pounding her hammer until almost dark. One night I heard her under a crawl space, talking to herself, but I couldn't hear what she was saying.

I find The Parents on the porch in folding chairs. Mom is using body-fat calipers on herself because first thing tomorrow, at Weigh-In (which on the program is listed as "No Room at the Weigh-In" . . . I *know*), her job will be the girls, getting their weight and BMI, while The Dad takes care of the boys. Mom is practicing on herself, pinching this tiny little bit of brown skin between her tank top and her jeans. Her hair is all caught up with a clip on top of her head and she looks pretty, younger than she has ever looked since she lost weight and got all buffed out, but then her face looks older. No, not older, just worried, maybe, like a face that has spent too much time looking down at the floor. The Dad is in one of his own T-shirt designs, which has a picture of the usual wavy-haired, blue-eyed Jesus, only all muscled out and wearing boxing gloves and these red satin Everlast shorts. The caption says, *Jesus, TKO Kings.* The Dad lifts his fake glasses to rub his eyes, and puts his hand on top of the stack of ledger sheets and printouts, like they are wearing him out, wearing him down. Maybe Jesus should be holding a pencil and a calculator instead. The Dad looks up at me and sighs.

"All set, sport? Our guests arrive in the morning."

"All set," I tell him. It's weird, that word *sport*. He used to call me that all the time when we were out in the surf or he was watching me learn to pop up on the long board, and it seemed right, back then. Now it just seems like some leftover thing, something abandoned on the beach. And the fact that he still uses it is just forced, kinda. Like, maybe, if he were still sitting out under a big umbrella all the time with zinc on his nose, like he hadn't noticed everything had changed.

"That's super," he says. He says stuff like this more and more as camp season approaches, but during the winter he hardly talks that way at all. I glance at Mom and she shakes her head a little bit, just enough for me to see. I think some of her got left behind at the beach too.

"Listen, Dad," I say, "I need to head into town. Can I take the van?" *Can I have a drink of water? Would you like some gum?* The key is nonchalance.

He runs his hand through his black curls. "Into town? You just did a load for me yesterday. Did you forget something?"

I could lie, but I don't.

"No," I tell him. "I want to go see someone."

He starts shaking his head before I have the words out. "Sorry, sport, that van is official biz only. And you aren't allowed to drive."

I feel my face heat up. "So, I can drive for you, but not for me?"

He calmly stacks up the ledger books and sets them on the little table off to the side. When he starts acting calm, you know he's getting mad. "You weren't driving for me yesterday, son. You were driving for Sonshine Valley, driving for the Lord."

"I don't think the Lord cares if we have nine hundred plastic cups and a sumo wrestler suit for Activities Day."

"Eliot, I don't like—"

"Sweetie?" Mom interrupts him. "What's her name?" I look at her, expecting more interrogation, but instead she is smiling, like I'm bringing her the first good news she's heard in years.

"Cal," I say, and it sounds strange, saying it out loud after saying it silently to myself a thousand times. "Her name is Cal, for Calliope."

"Is she pretty? I bet she is," she says.

"Cal?" The Dad says. "That girl who was out here with that woman?"

"Yes, she is pretty. She's . . . amazing." For a half second I am with her on the slide again, remembering one little detail I hadn't before . . . that when we went over the first bump, she let go of my leg to grab my hand, squeezing like she was scared we might just fly up into the air and never make it back.

The Dad screws up his face. "I don't think those are our kind of people, Eliot. I mean, her mother, what was her name? She was wearing about eight earrings in one ear."

"How many earrings do our kind of people wear?" I say.

"That's not the point."

"Sweetie, go take the van, have fun." Mom smiles again, twirling the calipers in her fingers.

"He's not taking my van."

"I thought it was the Lord's van," I say.

For half a second he looks stung, like I'd just reached across and hit him, and I know I've overstepped. My whole face is hot, like I can feel my pulse in my cheeks, in my forehead.

"Do you know what that girl's mother does out there at that Renaissance Faire? She plays a prostitute, letting men grope her so she'll get a bigger tip." He shakes his head. "If that makes me a prude, so be it."

"She's not a prostitute, Dad." I hear my own voice get louder. "She's a wench, like a serving wench, in a tavern."

"Taverns, wenches . . ."

"Dad, it's just a *character*, like some people are knights and some are kings, or whatever. I mean, God, the ninth grade took a field trip there last year. I don't think it's exactly evil."

"Don't take the Lord's name in vain."

"Jay, please," my mother says to him.

He looks at her, a long time, then leans back in his chair and takes a breath. "Just tell me one thing, son. Is Cal a Christian?"

I shake my head. "I don't know."

"Then it's safe to say she isn't. Eliot, you don't get this, but I really am watching out for you."

"Well, you'll like this part. Her boss is a Jewish carpenter."

He looks up at me, probably startled to hear his own bumper sticker repeated back to him. His other bumper sticker says, IN CASE OF RAPTURE THIS VEHICLE WILL BE UNOCCUPIED.

"Did she say that?"

"It's just a joke, Dad." Used to be it was always jokes, the three of us, teasing, popping towels at one another after using the beach shower to wash the sand off. I remember one time when we were on the beach in the fall, wrapped up in blankets and sweatshirts and sitting on coolers around a driftwood fire, and Mom said that everyone had to tell about something memorable that happened when they were teenagers, no fair telling something they'd told before. She told about one time she worked at the shopping center as one of Santa's elves all dressed in felt clothes, and she could never get the Polaroid camera to work and kept saying *damn* every time it messed up, and got fired after some three-year-old told Santa she wanted a damn Barbie Dream House. Then Dad told about the night of his senior prom when he and David Tucker had rolled up their rented tuxedo pants at three in the morning and took the rods from the trunk of the Impala and went casting in the surf because blues were running, fishing all night in their big bow ties and ruffled shirts. And with both stories they were laughing so much they could hardly get the words out, and then Dad kept teasing me, asking me to tell him what happened when I was a teenager, laughing because I was only eight years old, telling Mom that he believed I'd gone senile, that I couldn't remember one thing that happened during my formative teen years. And he kept asking and the fire was so warm against the night, and my face hurt from laughing so much, and the night grew darker and colder but they only stoked the fire and poured hot cocoa from this silver thermos and acted like we never needed to be anywhere else but right there. I want to remind him of that night, how he used to laugh before all of us got caught up in God and money, tell him that *right* now Cal is my memorable thing, the thing that happened to me.

"Maybe he used to be a carpenter," I say. "Now he just cooks ribs."

He just looks at me. "You can stand there and mock everything I believe in, everything that your life is made out of. That's your choice." For a minute he just looks at his hands on his lap.

"Dad, I didn't—"

"I'll be fair, son. Invite this Calliope to Spirit Night, let us get to know her a little bit, okay? But the van is mine, Eliot, and you are too young to be driving on dates, and you can't have it, I'm sorry."

I nod and walk back off the porch, walking blindly over the bridge and past the few geese that remain in our pond.

Thou shalt not steal is maybe the best Commandment, because it's pretty straightforward. I mean, so is the one about killing, but how many people are ever really tempted by that one, anyway? Some of the others are just strange, like coveting your neighbor's ass. I mean, huh? We don't even have neighbors. And bearing false witness, some people say that's like lying, but it sounds more like a courtroom thing, like something on TV with lawyers, when you take the oath, then sit behind the microphone. But everyone steals something, don't they? Or is at least tempted to? Denny Reese stole a microphone from the band room at school, and he took it home and didn't know what to do with it and so he just buried it under the porch. I know people steal typing paper or Post-it notes from the office, or they fudge on their taxes or they keep the wrong change they get back at Wal-Mart. So, it's a good Commandment because it covers a lot of ground, applies to most everyone.

I once stole some Slim Jims and a Spider-Man PEZ dispenser from a 7-Eleven, and the next day I felt so guilty that in chapel at school I went forward during the altar call and got prayed over, even though I was thinking that God probably didn't sweat Slim Jims and PEZ too much. And those were the only things I ever stole.

Until right now.

The spare key for the van stays in a little magnetic box hidden up under the wheel well, in case we ever lock ourselves out. I wait for The Parents to head over to the cafeteria, make sure they aren't coming back out, make sure Peto is off somewhere on the riding mower, and in a few seconds I'm in the van and heading out the gravel road. I'm so stupid, I turn down the radio, like that's going to keep me from getting busted, and I slink down a little in the seat and I check the rearviews like nineteen times before I even get to the road, and then I hit the asphalt and start breathing again.

It's the first week of the Faire, and I forgot how crowded it gets. I have to park way down the road from the parking lot, and when I pull over, the van lurches sideways, almost sliding over into the ditch. I run all the way up the road and my hand is still stamped from before because Cal told me not to wash it off, and I flash that at the gate and run inside, run around all these people in their long dresses and bodices and cloaks and chain mail, and then the regular people in their polo shirts and fanny packs, past a circle where two guys are whacking each other with wooden swords, until I finally find the Cloven Hoof booth, all that sweet smoke pouring out from under the tent. Abel is there, wearing an apron that says ASK ME ABOUT OUR KOSHER PEACH COBBLER! and wiping his face on the arm of his T-shirt, knocking crooked his Red Sox baseball cap.

He looks up. "Eliot, right?"

"Yes, sir."

"'Sir,' huh? What did I ever do to you? It's 'Abel,' okay?"

"Okay. Where's Cal?"

He puts his tongs aside and wipes his hands and looks up at me, and for a second I wish I'd remembered my sunglasses. "What's wrong, Eliot?"

"Nothing, I just want to find her."

"Nothing? You know, cooking ribs gives one a certain amount of insight into human psychology."

"I didn't know that."

"It's a joke."

I smile a little. "I didn't know that either."

"Man, tough crowd. Eliot, I think Cal is at the house still.

She was here late helping me set up. If something's wrong, maybe I can help."

No, nothing's wrong, only that my father is right now calling the highway patrol and sheriff's office to report his son as a car thief. "I'm fine," I tell him. The sweat on my back feels cool and sticky. Abel has an old, faded, smeary tattoo on his arm, and just to change the subject I point at it, ask him what it is.

"Yin/yang," he says. "A hippie icon, from back in the day when I thought I was one. A hippie, I mean, not an icon. And it is, but then getting a tattoo is so bourgeois and right-wing, at least then, when, you know, only the military had them, so I was embracing and alienating my cultural base in the time it took to get stuck by a bunch of needles. I'm not making sense, am I?"

I smile. "You're trying, that's the important part."

He throws back his head and lets loose the biggest laugh I've ever seen. "You are okay, Eliot. She done good." He looks at me again, and before I can open my mouth, he says, "Go find her."

I'm a mile down the road before I realize that I don't know where I'm going, I forgot to ask Abel where the house is, and that I'm just driving. Every time a car comes over a ridge or around a curve, I tense up, expecting to see blue lights turning and flashing, and by now the back of my shirt is sticking to the vinyl seat. When I picture The Parents and how worried and upset and disappointed they must be, I feel like all the air has been sucked out of the van. *Think,* I tell myself, and my brain digs up enough to remind me that Cal said the house was near the Cloven Hoof and that it was made of stone. Like a castle, she said.

It only takes three circles around three different blocks before I find the house, and I leave the van running at the curb, run up, knock on the door, knock again, and no one answers. Standing there, sweating, hands shaking, I try out every swearword I ever learned and glance over to the garage, look up, and there she is. Her face is framed inside a little square window, and she looks out and then down and her head and curls are moving a little bit. And I know right away that she's standing at the sink washing dishes. It's the same way anyone looks out the window when they wash dishes, looking far, far off. The wooden steps on the side of the garage take me up to her door in about two seconds, and she answers with her hands wet up past the wrists and a towel thrown across her shoulder, and she is barefoot, in cutoffs and a T-shirt with a picture of dogs playing poker.

"Eliot?" she says, and I realize from her expression that I must look a little bit crazy by now.

"Hi."

"Hi," she says, and her face softens.

"I have the van," I say. "Come ride with me."

"I have to be at the tent at four."

"I'll get you there. I'll even get you there at three fifty-nine."

She laughs, tosses the cloth into the sink. "Where are we going?"

"Nowhere," I say. "Anywhere. Everywhere."

She laughs again. "I don't have time for all of those. Can we just go everywhere for today?"

"Of course," I say, and step back enough to pull the screen door open wide.

Eliot's John the Baptist Barbecue Sauce

2 tablespoons vegetable oil, like soy, corn, or peanut

½ medium onion, chopped

6 cloves garlic, minced

pinch of crushed red pepper

1 tablespoon tomato paste

1 (28-ounce) can whole peeled tomatoes (with puree), pureed

¾ cup red wine vinegar

¾ cup honey

½ cup grape jelly

1½ teaspoon kosher salt

freshly ground black pepper

Heat the oil in a medium saucepan over medium-high heat. Add the onion and cook, stirring, until lightly browned, about 4 minutes.

Add the garlic and crushed pepper and cook, stirring frequently, until fragrant, about 45 seconds.

Add the tomato paste and cook, stirring, until lightly browned, about 1 minute more.

Add the tomatoes, vinegar, honey, grape jelly, and salt, and bring to a boil. Lower the heat and simmer, uncovered, stirring occasionally, until deep red in color and reduced to about 4 cups, about 25 minutes.

Season with pepper. Use immediately or store, covered, in the refrigerator for up to 3 days or freeze for up to 1 month.

Yield: about 4 cups

9 calliope

We ride in silence for a few minutes, but it's not that someone-better-say-something silence. This is the soft green kind. The kind that makes you think of new grass and sprinklers and lemonade. The kind you have after you've known each other for a million years, but that can't be right because we've just met. So, there must be another kind. Eliot keeps strumming his fingers on the steering wheel like he's nervous, but at least his face is relaxed. When I first opened the door and saw him standing there on the porch, his eyes looked crazed and I thought for a minute there he was going to tell me something really bad, but then he just smiled and asked me to go for a drive.

"So, what are you hauling?" I ask, twisting myself in my seat to see into the back of the van. Plastic bags and boxes are stacked everywhere.

"Stuff for the camp. We start up tomorrow."

"The Bible Outlet," I read aloud from the side of one of the boxes. "What's that? Overstock? Irregulars?"

"Just extras in case the campers forget theirs."

Eliot doesn't catch my sarcasm, so I continue. "So, maybe in some of them Jesus is spelled with a *p*, so someone goes through life telling everyone that Jepus is their savior." I am afraid I have gone too far, because Eliot doesn't smile. He just keeps staring into the rearview mirror.

We ride in silence again, but now it's the other kind. The black kind. The awkward, maybe-this-car-ride-wasn't-such-a-good-idea kind. The kind you sit through at the dinner table because your parents are trying to make a good showing by having a family dinner. And I keep thinking maybe I should say something or do something, but then Eliot smiles at me.

"Jepus," he says. "That's funny."

"You seem a bit distracted," and I am thinking, *Good job, Dr. Obvious.*

"Your apartment looks nice," he says, checking the rearview again. "Well, what I could see of it from the doorway."

I decide to play along for a few more minutes. "You saw most of it. It's not big."

"Bigger than my cabin," he says.

"Okay, most good-sized lunch boxes are bigger than your cabin." Again Eliot stares in the rearview for longer than he should.

"Yeah . . . lunch boxes," he says, finally pulling his gaze away from the mirror and back to me.

"You running from the law?" Eliot jerks as if I hit him. "Whoa," I say, putting my hand on his arm. "Tell me what's going on."

The silence comes again, but this one is red. Hot and pulsing and frightening. Like something bad is going to happen, like your whole world is going to change and nothing you have taken for granted is going to be around anymore. That kind. I take a deep breath and it comes in at a rush as if I have been holding my breath forever.

"I—" he begins, but something in the rearview mirror distracts him. I look in the side mirror and see a white van behind us about twenty yards back. Eliot slows and starts to pull toward the shoulder. The van honks at us before speeding past. I notice that Eliot's hands are white, clutching the wheel and shaking.

"Just tell me," I say, keeping my hand on his arm the whole time. "Remember? No secrets. Whatever it is, we can handle it." He looks at me as if seeing me for the first time today. As if he is remembering something. I nod at the question he doesn't even ask.

He opens his mouth, but what comes out isn't actually English, but rather an impression of English spoken by someone jacked up on five bowls of Count Chocula, flying at the speed of light, who is trying to compress a lifetime of words into seven seconds. I catch "underage," "kill me," "stolen," and "vanilla bean," before I hold up my hand.

"Okay, as far as I can tell, you aren't really the son of a famous motivational speaker and evangelist, but are actually working for a very obscure wing of an organized-crime family who makes its money trafficking stolen vanilla beans in order to sell them to underage children. And, something has gone wrong and you are worried that you are being targeted for a hit." I smile at him and for a minute he doesn't move at all. He just stares forward at the road disappearing under the van. Then he starts laughing. One of those silent laughs that builds. Soon we are both laughing, tears running down our cheeks, trying to catch our breaths.

"That was remarkably close," he says, still smiling.

It's quiet for a while again, but this time it's one of those yellowy orange silences that makes you think of birthday cake and brightly colored balloons. Eliot takes his hand off the wheel and rests it on my leg, right where my shorts end, and I can feel the heat from each of his fingers and the slightly sticky feeling of his palm, damp with sweat. I watch as they spread a bit across the top of my thigh, dividing my pale skin into unfinished triangles. I am studying the feeling his hand is giving me so hard that I almost don't notice as he slows and pulls into a gravel parking lot.

"Here we are," he says, shifting the van into park and turning off the engine. The building in front of us seems on the verge of falling in on itself, but the sign out front is freshly painted. HOT LICKS. COLD ICE CREAM AND HOT JAZZ. "It's too early for music, but not for ice cream," he says.

After a brief argument about the merits of vanilla versus chocolate, we are seated on the back deck, two dripping waffle cones in our hands. His chocolate. Mine vanilla.

"They say that's the largest duck made completely out of chocolate," he says, referring to the mascot just inside the front entrance. "The owners started out to build a moose, but some candy store up north had one already."

"You ready to tell me yet?" I ask. He keeps taking little bites of ice cream, making pockmarks in his scoop. "Doesn't that make your teeth cold?"

"Do you always change subjects like that?" he asks.

"Do you always answer questions with a question?"

"Do you always have a smart answer for everything?"

"Yes," I say, pursing my lips, but I can't keep from smiling.

"Okay, smarty, tell me something. What would you say if I told you that I wasn't supposed to be out today. That I'm not supposed to have the van. That I'm not supposed to be driving at all because I'm only fifteen."

"I'd say you must have a good reason for doing it."

"Well, yeah," Eliot says, taking a few more bites. The silence comes again. This one starts out soft baby blue, expectant and waiting. But, then he looks at me and the color shifts, brightening and glowing into a slowly shifting silver. "I had a good reason."

The back door bangs open and half a dozen tourists stomp out onto the deck. We smile at each other again before going back to work on our cones.

"What's your favorite color?" I ask.

"Orange."

"Favorite pizza topping?"

"Mushrooms."

"Water with lemon or no?" I ask, dumping the nub of my cone in the trash.

"With."

"Chess or backgammon?" I continue as we walk back through the shop and out to the van.

"Backgammon," he says, unlocking my side and closing my door. I breathe hard on the passenger-side window and draw a lazy heart on the fogged glass and link it with another and another until a chain of them disappears into the glass.

"Rain or snow?" I ask as he slides into his seat.

"Rain. What's with all the questions?" he asks, pushing the key into the ignition.

"I just think I should get to know as much as I can about someone before I let him kiss me."

"Really?" he asks, leaning his head against the headrest and staring forward through the windshield. "You thinking about letting me kiss you?"

"I'm thinking about it," I say, looking at his hands, one rest-ing on his leg and the other on the steering wheel. They look so strong, like they could hold just about anything.

"So what else do you want to know?" he asks, shifting to face me. I get that same buzzy feeling in my head like I had the first time I ever talked to him. "Nothing?" he asks, leaning toward me. I shake my head slightly, leaning forward to meet him. "You sure?" he asks, his mouth about an inch from mine. Another shake. "Positive?" he asks, but then his lips are against mine and I can taste chocolate from his ice cream and peppermint from his gum and I'm pretty sure that those two flavors will be welded into my brain as Eliot-flavored. The kiss seems like it lasts forever and no time at all. And we stay like that, our mouths slowly moving together, his hand in my hair and his breath hot on my face. The sound of the door and laughter makes us spring apart, but it's only the Interrupting Tourists again. Eliot smiles at me before turning the key.

We start home, his hand on my leg again and my hand over his. We are quiet, but this time it's the dark blue kind, the midnight kind, the sink-in-until-you-lose-yourself kind. And somewhere in the deep blue silence, I can taste the sweetness of mint chocolate, and feel the gentle tug of fingers in my hair, and hear the quiet thud of my own heart. Lost in the blue, I squeeze Eliot's hand as it rests on my leg and he squeezes back, not letting go even as we bump over a broken bit of road and slow down for a long, hard curve.

✦　✦　✦

"So did he find you?" Abel asks as I lift my apron from the back table. "Wait, don't tell me. That look on your face is the only answer I need." I watch as he flips a long course of ribs and uses a paintbrush to dab them with sauce.

"When are you going to teach me to make that?" I ask, pointing at the pot bubbling away at the back of the grill.

"When I feel you are worthy."

"When will that be?" I ask, but he doesn't respond. Something past my shoulder has caught his eye and it takes a minute before he can pull his gaze back to my face. "What is it?" I say, turning to look toward the beer tent.

"Nothing . . . I just—" he begins, but not before I see. I turn back to the grill and jab at the ribs with more force than I intend, breaking the rack in half and sending grease into the flames, making them flare up against the meat. "Hey," Abel says, catching my elbow before I can give the ribs another poke. "What did they ever do to you?"

I feel my eyes go hot and I close them against the smoke and unwanted tears. "I don't like him," I say, pushing my hair away from my face with my forearm. I hate the whiny tone in my voice and the petulance of my words.

"Phi's okay," Abel says, taking the tongs and offering me a clean paper towel in exchange. I squint at him and he smiles. "I mean, if you like self-centered, overly muscled alpha males."

I nod and wipe at my eyes. "Have you seen his license plates?" I ask.

"Have you seen his tattoo?" Abel asks. I shake my head. "It's of a jouster on a horse." I can't help smiling. "I mean, I think it's actually him. He has himself tattooed on his shoulder."

"That's pretty bad," I say, balling up the paper towel and aiming it toward the trash can at the back of the tent. I miss. "Why can't she just find someone nice?" I ask, taking the tongs back from Abel. I poke at the ribs more gently this time, as Abel walks to the front of the tent to begin taking orders for the dinner rush. Hours pass and the mindless work of cooking and serving fills my brain.

"Let's pack it up," Abel finally says, flipping the front of the tent down. "You meeting up with Eliot tonight?" he asks, stretching his arms overhead. I hear his spine crack twice, then three times.

I shake my head. "It might be a while before I see Eliot again," I say, turning the dials on the grills to *Off*. Abel cocks his head at me. "His parents," I add, and that seems like enough of an answer. I start scrubbing at the scabs of grease and meat that the ribs have left behind. It's just like Delores to somehow take over my brain like this. Now when I think of kissing, instead of Eliot, I think of her pressed against Phi this afternoon, his hand on the small of her back and her leaning against him on tiptoes. Now instead of the soft, velvety blueness of Eliot's kiss, I am left with a hard, sharp magenta memory of Delores's kiss. A kiss that seems like a warning of some kind, but one I can't quite decipher.

"If you want to wait, I'll give you a ride all the way home," Abel says, putting the truck in park behind the restaurant. "I just need to drop a couple of things off. It won't take more than a few minutes."

"I think I'll just walk," I tell him, sliding out of the truck. I feel shaky, like I haven't slept enough or have had too much coffee to drink. I feel Abel's eyes on me as I walk down the alley and turn onto the sidewalk. He's worried about me, I know. Something I'm not used to. It feels uncomfortable and nice all at the same time. Like a wool sweater. It makes me itchy, but I feel all warm inside.

I pass the darkened shops on the way to the apartment. The coffee shop is still peopled with single men reading thick novels and couples lacing their fingers together over their lattes. I imagine that the elves are working away as I pass the shoe store. A woman stands leaning on her broom in front of La Paperie, her eyes gazing through me as I walk by. At home I stand in the driveway, watching, as shadows move across the windows. There's a candle lit on the table in the garden and I can hear guitar music dripping through the doorway.

"Grab the wine, would you?" Delores calls behind her as she steps out onto the landing. She is carrying a platter in one hand and holding her skirt away from her feet with the other. She's barefoot and her hair hangs down her back, wet and straight.

"Red or white?" a male voice asks from within.

"Both," Delores calls, stepping off the bottom step and into the garden. She looks toward where I am standing, but I am hidden in the near darkness. She pulls a grape from the bunch on the platter and pops it into her mouth, closing her eyes while she chews.

"Where's the corkscrew?" the voice asks from above. She shakes her head and starts back up the stairs. Phi steps out onto the landing, holding a bottle in one hand.

"You can't find anything," Delores says, trying to slide past him and back into the apartment.

"I think I'm doing okay," Phi says, placing his hand against her back and following her through the doorway. I hear her laughter as he pushes the door shut with his foot. As I watch the shadows move across the windows again, I have only one thought and it's so strong that I have no choice but to follow it. I start toward the garage, hoping that one of the bikes has a light on it.

"What are you still doing out here?" I turn, and see Abel walking up the driveway toward me. "I thought you'd be nearly in bed by now." I don't move, caught between my decision and Abel's arrival. "What's that?" he asks pointing toward the garden. I turn and start walking toward the garage again. I decide that light or no, I'm taking one of the bikes. Abel stands watching me as I struggle with the garage door. "Cal, what are you after?" he asks, putting his hand on the garage and keeping it from rolling up. "I mean, what's mine is yours, but at least tell me so I can help."

"I need to borrow a bike," I say, pulling on the handle again. He presses harder on the door, stopping it again.

"Cal, it's dark. You can't go out riding now."

"I have to get out. I have to—" And then the tears that I have been holding in all day come. They feel hot as they slide down my cheeks and drip from my chin. Abel stands looking at me and then at the ground and then up at the apartment above us. He closes his eyes for a moment and I know he understands.

"You running away?" he asks, smiling slightly at me, but it's only half a joke. "You might want to pack some food, get a jacket."

"Not away," I say. "To." And, once I say it, I realize it's true. "Just for a little while. I just can't go up there."

"Your mother will worry," he says, but more as a question than a statement.

I shake my head. "She won't. I'll be back before she notices."

"You can't ride a bike there," he says. "It's too dangerous after dark." He reaches into his pocket and pulls out his keys. "Let's go," he says, turning and walking back toward the street. I follow him back to the restaurant in silence. He unlocks the passenger-side door and walks around to the other side of the truck, then digs in his pockets again and climbs in behind the wheel. He hands me his cell phone and a handkerchief before sliding the key in the ignition.

"Thank you," I say, wiping my face. Abel pulls the truck out of the parking lot and aims it away from downtown and toward the hills.

"You call me if you need a ride back," he says, sliding through the traffic light that is only blinking yellow now. "Don't worry about waking me up. I don't sleep much, anyway."

"Are you sure?" I say softly. Abel nods. We ride in silence, and I can feel that spiky, shaky feeling falling away as we grow closer.

"I won't take you all the way up," Abel says, pulling to the side of the road and turning off his lights. "Something tells me these people don't much like surprises." I open my door and slide my feet to the ground. "Cal, you be careful, understand?"

I nod. "Thank you," I say again, bravely, trusting myself to speak.

The rumble of Abel's idling truck grows fainter as I walk up the road to the camp entrance. It's only when I almost reach the edge of the clearing that I hear the sound of tires in gravel as he turns the truck around to drive back to town.

Eliot's cabin is dark, and I start to wonder if maybe this was a bad idea after all. I almost chicken out, but decide I should at least go see if he's in there. The pine needles under my sneakers seem too loud in the darkness as I walk up to the nearest window. I cup my hands against the screen and peer into the darkness. His bed is empty, the sheets stretched tight across the bed.

"Damn it," I say aloud, dropping my hands to my sides.

"Yeah, you can't use that kind of language here." I turn and see Eliot standing there, not six inches in front of me. He's dressed only in flannel pants and flip-flops. A toothbrush and toothpaste dangle from his hand. "What are you—?"

"I needed you," I say, and that seems like answer enough, because he walks past me and holds the door to his cabin open.

Places You Have to Visit
If You Drive Cross-Country

by Cal

Presque Isle to Houlton, Maine—Maine Solar System Model
The Maine Solar System Model is a scale model (1 mile = 1 astronomical unit, approximately 1:93,000,000) of the solar system, beginning at the Houlton visitor information center (I-95 at US 1) with a 1-inch-diameter Pluto, and extending northward 40 miles to the University of Maine at Presque Isle campus and a 50-foot-diameter sun.

Mattapoisett, Massachusetts—Giant Sea Horse
On Route 6, an odd, faded bluish green sea horse, with some pink and yellow thrown in, surveys the center of town.

Frostburg, Maryland—God's Ark of Safety
In 1974, Pastor Richard Greene was repeatedly told by Jesus to build an ark by the interstate, and he commenced "The Rebuilding of Noah's Ark as a Last Day Witness to the World." The ark is not yet finished.

Paris, Texas—Jesus Wearing Cowboy Boots Grave
Paris has the world's largest cemetery, with 50,000-plus graves, including one headstone with Jesus wearing cowboy boots.

Santa Cruz, California—Santa Cruz Mystery Spot
Pseudoscientific anomaly, where the laws of gravity and physics go
haywire.

Saint Benedict, Oregon—World's Largest Hairball
The world's largest hairball is in the Mount Angel Abbey Museum
near Mount Angel. Weighing 2.5 pounds, it came from a hog's
stomach.

Salad of the Gods—Various Places
Poteet, Texas—Huge Strawberry
Cornelia, Georgia—Biggest Apple
Castroville, California—Giant Artichoke
Luling, Texas—Giant Watermelon
Olivia, Minnesota, and Dublin, Ohio—Gigantic Corn
Winlock, Washington—World's Largest Egg
Clermont, Florida—Giant Orange
Jonesboro, Maine—World's Largest Blueberry
Clanton, Alabama—Giant Peach
Seguin, Texas—Enormous Pecan

10 eliot

As we walk across the bridge, Cal lets go of my hand long enough to pick up some of the corn spilled from the gum-ball machine we have mounted on the railing. People buy the corn to feed the geese and carp. She drops a kernel into the water and the rings move out from it, then the one goose still awake swims over our way, the others asleep on the bank with their heads tucked under their wings.

"That one's me," she says, watching the goose swim under us then tip his head down into the water.

"You mean your constant craving for floating corn?"

She elbows me. "No, doofus. I mean awake in the middle of the night, solitary. I bet she's worrying about something, fretting until daylight."

"Yeah, if I thought those hunters might come back I'd be up all night too. And listen, you aren't solitary, not anymore." I take her hand and squeeze it, lace my fingers with hers.

She smiles and leans on the rail, her hair leaning with her, her bottle cap falling out of her tank top, swaying on its red string, and with it something else, flashing silver in the dark. I pick it up with my free hand. A locket, and it looks old, like something my grandmother wore when she was alive. And right in the middle, in this curly script, an engraved *E*.

"Nice *E*," I say. "I know it's not any of your initials."

"You know, I am still hungry, you did offer to feed me."

"What's the *E* for?"

She shakes her head full of curls, and even in the dim light I can see her blush. "*Eggs*," she says. "Scrambled. *Eggplant*. You know, egg-related stuff."

"You know, my name starts with an *E*."

She smiles and takes the locket from my fingers. "What's your name again?"

"Egbert," I tell her, and I get to watch her laugh again. "And I'm sorry, but I don't believe your egg story."

She kisses me, still blushing. "It stands for *elephantitis*, which is my favorite disease . . . no? It's for *eclipse*, for *electricity*, for *estuary*, for *epossum*, for—"

"'Epossum'? I think that's *opossum*. And you're in North Carolina now, so it's just *possum*."

"Yeah, on menus maybe, sure. But elsewhere there is a huge problem with the epossum. The northern woods are full of them."

"I'm sorry, I wasn't listening. You said something about someone being full of something?"

She laughs once more, kisses me, and it's a relief to see her happy again. When I first found her, outside my cabin, I was so surprised that I didn't even think to ask the right questions, or any questions. It was like she just materialized on my porch, beamed in. I took her inside, and she put her arms around me, her hands cold on my neck, and squeezed like she wanted to break me.

I held her, and let her breathe into the cup of my shoulder, and swallowed the toothpaste in my mouth. Her hands pressed into my back, and I felt her eyelashes flutter against my skin, her tears running down across my chest.

"What?" I whispered. "Tell me what happened." But she just kept shaking her head.

"I swear, sometimes I think I hate her," she whispered.

"Who?" I said, though I knew who she meant, the only "her" she could mean. I'd seen her mother around at the Faire, even met her once, and I wanted her to like me. I mean, I live at the Christian camp, and when I have to I can bust out the game-show-host smile, and parents always like me. Except, well, my own right now, with the van and all. And as much as I wanted that, I'd seen how Cal's mom was with her, always acting not so much like a mom, but almost like an older sister who maybe wanted to sneak out of the house at night and wanted little sis to cover for her, lie for her, make it right. And gripe all you want, but sometimes you just want your mom to be your mom.

She leaned back to look at me, small tears quivering on her eyelashes. "I don't want to hate anyone, Eliot."

"I know."

"It turns you black inside, one little corner at a time."

I nodded and used my thumb to wipe away her tears. "Tell her that," I said. "Or don't. But just because she runs around wearing baseball spikes doesn't mean you have to lie down and let her walk over you."

She looked at me. "Man, that was dumb." She started laughing, her eyes still wet.

"Yeah, but I was just making—"

"Okay, but that was *really* dumb."

I nodded. "Here at the camp, that's my job—bad counseling. Like this week, I'll be telling people that they have to think of themselves as giant LEGO kits, then just unsnap the unhappy parts and throw them back in the box."

"You're good at bad counseling," she said. "I'm semi-impressed."

"How did you get here?" I brushed her hair back with my knuckles.

"Well, when a man and woman fall in love . . ."

"No, goofball, how did you get here *tonight*?"

"Abel brought me, right before I could steal his bicycle." She slid her hands down to hold my hands, and I could see her sneaking glances at my chest, suddenly very aware that I wasn't wearing a shirt, wishing I'd saved my push-ups for night instead of the morning.

"Enough stolen vehicles for one week," I told her.

"What happened with that?"

"I'll tell you later," I said, and shook my head.

"That bad, huh?"

"Does Abel have a little Christmas tree hanging from his rearview that smells like garlic and chili powder?"

"So you're saying I stink. Nice move, Eliot."

"No," I said, "you just smell like Cal." My voice dropped down to a whisper. "My Cal." I pulled her against me, let my hand slide up along her neck and disappear into her curls, filling my fingers with them, then leaned down and kissed her, our mouths melding, warm, moving, the sounds of our breaths blending and deepening in the silence of my little room. She moved back from me, her face flushed, my own face full of a warmth that spread down to my chest, down through me.

"We should probably go outside, you know, and"—she glanced around the room—"check on the trees, or something."

"The trees."

"Yes. Like make sure they aren't on fire or anything."

"If I said something about it being warm enough for a fire, that would be a really bad line, wouldn't it?" I smiled at her.

"Well, after the baseball spikes and telling me I stink, at least you'd be consistent."

I laughed. "Listen, you hurried over here. Did you eat?"

"I ate lunch."

"But no dinner? I'm cooking—what would you like for dinner?"

"Breakfast," she said.

And so she watches me, sitting against the wall inside the cafeteria, while I open the big stainless doors and find eggs and bacon and rye bread and a potato, and while I find enough coffee left in the big Bunn-O-Matic to heat in the microwave, with only the light above the stove to see by. We talk while I'm cooking, and I tell Cal how totally busted I was when I got back with the van, how The Dad has started writing down the mileage on the odometer *every* day, after every trip, to make sure I'm not running it up if I go into town. I feel like one of those criminals who gets to stay home but has to wear an electronic anklet. Sometimes I want to rip the odometer out of the dash, and the clock too, and just drive . . . drive with Cal beside me and there is no distance, no time, just going and going with her beside me. But then I realize I don't really have anywhere to go, and it's not the going that counts, anyway, it's having her with me. If you're in love, everywhere is the same. What I don't tell her is the big lecture I got about how "those people" are a bad influence on me. I get the feeling sometimes that The Dad doesn't even want to count himself as people anymore. He is something different, better. Cal puts the rye bread in the toaster and finds the butter and jam, and tells me about Phi and the way her mother acts around him and how he has a tattoo of himself on his arm.

I dish up the plates and we pull the high metal stools up to the stainless counter, eating by stove light, the tree peepers outside making slow noises. We eat a few minutes in silence, just scooping up the eggs and scraping jam onto the bread, and there is something about that silence that lets me know Cal wants it to stretch out a few minutes, no talking.

"I mean," she says finally, as if there weren't a lull, "that's a perfect symbol for the kind of guy she likes, you know? He has a tattoo of himself, and his tattoo self has a tattoo of Phi, and that tattoo has a tattoo. It's like restroom mirrors, just this infinity of nothing. That's what she wants, and keeps chasing."

"Maybe she's lonely," I say. "I'm not defending her, but . . ." I shrug, thinking of my own mom and how lonely she has seemed, for years. Soon, I think, I won't be able to remember her being any other way.

"I know, Eliot. She's searching. I mean, who isn't? But it's like when you're lost in the woods . . ."

"You know, you're like a superhero," I tell her. "Analogy Girl." She finishes her coffee and I pour her some more. Extra cream, a little sugar.

She smiles, flexes her biceps. ". . . you're lost in the woods, what's the dumbest mistake you can make?" she says.

I stack the plates together and rip a paper towel in two for our napkins, something I forgot before. The big school clock above the sink clicks to the next minute, going on one in the morning. "Wander around," I say. "Don't stay put; don't light a fire."

"Good job."

"Yeah, I was a Boy Scout for three days."

"And wander around is exactly what Delores does." We turn off the stove light and sit on the cool floor, in a patch of light shining through the window. Cal takes my hand. "She's lonely, she's lost, and that would end if she'd just stay put, let people find her. But she always moves off, again and again."

There is a sudden knot in my stomach. "Will she move off? Take you?"

She nods, not looking at me. "She could."

I shake my head. "I don't like that." I feel like something is pressing on my chest.

"I don't like it either," she says, and turns to look at me, frowning. I cup her face in my palm and kiss her, her mouth warm and salty, the moonlight shining on half her face. I kiss her mouth, her cheek, her hair.

"Don't go," I say.

"You want me to stay right here, sitting against this wall?" She tips her head back and leans against it.

"Yes, until we figure something else out," I say.

"Well, as long as you keep me fed. If you have to pick a wall, pick one in the kitchen, right? I mean—"

I put my finger to her lips. "You have to hush a minute so I can tell you something."

"What?" she says, bites my finger.

I look at her. "I love you."

She gets quiet, the kind of quiet that sinks into her, softens her. "Well, that works out," she finally says, her voice deeper and breathless, her eyes moist, "because I love you too." She turns, leans against my arm, and settles into me.

The school clock shows 4:00 a.m. when the fluorescent lights snap on, the door bangs shut, and I realize we've been sleeping. I jolt upright, but Cal only stirs a little bit, my arm asleep beneath her, my heart wobbling in my chest. In the half a second it takes my eyes to focus, I see Mom standing there in her sweats, and all I can think for a second is why is she wearing her rubber gardening boots? Then it quickly becomes apparent I have bigger worries.

"*Eliot*," she says, in what I can only think of as a loud whisper. "What are you *doing*? Where have you *been*?"

"It's my fault," Cal says, sitting up. "I dragged him out here, to feed me. God, that sounds bad." She shakes her head. "Wait, I'm sorry I said 'God,' I just . . ." Her face is red, her hands shaking.

Mom snaps off the light, and lets go a deep, long breath. She sits on the floor across from us and raises the flashlight in her hand. "I should bop you both with this," she says. "I've been looking *everywhere*. I guess I should be happy to find you here, I mean . . ." She lets the thought go.

"We ate and we fell asleep, Mom," I say.

"Yes, I was able to assemble the clues," she says, then surprises me by smiling.

"How did you know to even look for me? It's not like you wake up much at—"

"I got a call, from some man named Abel, a friend of yours?" She looks at Cal. "I'm Linda," she says, and shakes hands. "Anyway, I thought, wonderful, now we are getting phone calls from biblical figures, but turns out he was just worried about you, Cal. Then Eliot wasn't in his cabin. This was literally the last place I looked." She leans back against the stainless counter and pulls her knees up, hugging them, like she plans to sit there all night.

"What about Dad?" I say. "After the whole van thing, I don't think this—"

"He's asleep," she says, looking away.

"But the phone—"

"He's asleep in his office," she says. "Again." She blinks her eyes fast and starts acting like the flashlight is the most interesting thing in the world.

"Mom?"

"Honey, it's fine. Your father is working very hard. He's just tired." I nod, watching her, squeezing Cal's hand. At the same time I'm thinking that all Cal ever talks about is her mother, like her father doesn't even exist.

Mom turns to Cal. "You know, if you were fat, you could just come live here for the next few weeks. I think this one might like that." She lightly punches my knee.

"Would you like it if I were fat, Eliot?" Cal says. "Because there's an entire Godiva store at the mall with my name on it."

Mom laughs. This is the first time I have ever heard Mom use the word *fat*. Whenever The Dad is around, I have to remember to use words like *differently weighted* or *metabolically challenged*.

"Sweetie?" Mom says to Cal, touching her wrist. "Why don't I call your mother and let her know you're here and safe?"

"We don't have a phone," Cal says. "Would it be okay if you just dropped me off?"

"Won't you be in trouble? Do you want me to talk to her?"

She shakes her head. "No, it's okay."

Mom nods. "I hear you're coming to Spirit Night."

"I am?"

"Yes," I tell her. "If you want to." And she nods like she has no idea what she's agreeing to, which is probably right. My image of last year's Spirit Night is of eighty cheering fat people throwing symbolic bags of Fritos on a giant bonfire.

"Okay then," Mom says. "Let's get you home."

When the orange buses full of campers show up, The Dad has blaring through the loudspeakers this Christian country song called "Jesus Built the Highway and I Drove the Car." I watch them stepping off, carrying their duffel bags and backpacks and portable CD players, thinking that if I have to hear this song twice I am going to become seriously depressed. I can barely keep my eyes open after the night before, and all day long I have thought about our midnight breakfast, and her face in the half moonlight, and the fact that she told me she loves me. She did tell you that, I keep telling myself. Then I run over the whole scene again in my head, and I slow down the tape right at that point, to make sure I got it right, that she didn't say *like* or didn't slip a *don't* in there somewhere. And again and again I see her, the way her whole body, her face, softened into quietness, and again she says, *because I love you too,* which would be way better than the song lyrics blasting out over the camp, the ones about *Jesus in a hard hat, cranking up the big Cat, paving all the streets with gold. . . .* The singer wrings about three syllables out of the word *gold,* then lots of twangy guitars kick in. Pretty terrible.

I always feel bad for the campers. They are all about my age, some a little younger, some as old as twenty-one, and they always look scared and relieved at the same time. Like they have just crash-landed on their home planet—the crash was scary, but it's good to be home. And I think home for them probably just means a place where they are the normal ones, for once, where the boys can talk to girls or take off their shirts at the pool, normal stuff they have never done. They look around, their faces pink, the space under their eyes sweaty and hollow looking. Some of them dress in really hip stuff, with baggy pants and chain wallets, like if they just dress the part they will fit right in. But they never will. Even at my school, where teasing is treated as a sin, they never do. One boy, a first as far as I can remember, steps off the bus, puts his duffel on the ground, then kneels on it and starts to pray, hands clasped. The Dad walks out with his bullhorn crackling, saying, *It's a new day that the Lord has made,* the same way he wakes them up every morning. I watch him talk to them, watch the boy finish up his prayer as if no one else were around, watch the overweight girls nervously tucking their hair behind their ears, holding on to big Snoopys and pillows. And this year, for the first time I can remember, Mom is not there, not standing beside him in the Lycra workout clothes meant to show off her abs because, The Dad always tells her, you have to give those girls a model to strive for. She's not there, and all I can think about is last night, after we took the van out at almost five in the morning to drop Cal at home, driving through the streets where nothing moved except a street sweeper, where all the traffic lights were green, and how after I watched Cal tiptoe up her wooden stairs Mom said that she seemed like a sweet girl, like the perfect girl for me, and then I turned to look at her, her eyes bloodshot. She sighed, like she was too tired to make it back home, still wearing her sweats and the green gardening boots.

"Eliot?" she said, her voice quiet.

"Yes?"

"Sometime after Spirit Night, let's play hooky."

"From camp?"

She flicked her eyes at me. "If Cal were here she would say, 'well, duh.' Yes, honey, from camp."

"Won't Dad get mad? That's like the busiest week."

She nodded, pulled the shifter into drive, and started down the street. "Yes," she said, "your father will get mad."

I waited for her to excuse it or something, but that's all she said.

"Can I bring Cal?"

"You can bring all of Asheville, as far as I'm concerned."

"Okay. Where are we going?"

She smiled, and the tiredness left her face for a minute. "Only one place I want to be," she said. "And that's Carolina Beach."

The Ten Commandments, as Posted on the Sonshine Valley Cafeteria Wall

BY ELIOT

I. Thou shalt honor thy health and happy, happy thoughts above all else.

II. Thou shalt not work the vending machines: therein lieth the way of madness.

III. Thou shalt not steal bites from thy neighbor's plate.

IV. Thou shalt not eat when thine eye lusteth but when thy stomach doth supplicate for sustenance.

V. Thou shalt sup chiefly on the fruits of the earth, the grains and vegetables thereof, on the fowl of the air and the fish of the seven seas, whence cometh not doughnuts.

VI. Thou shalt not eat when thou art feeling sad, for food is not a medicine unto the soul. Thou shalt hug thyself instead.

VII. Thou shalt take exercise daily; for why hast thou sinew and bone, legs and sneakers?

VIII. Thou shalt not eat in front of thy TV.

IX. Thou shalt delight in every good word and good song and good day.

X. Thou shalt keep these Commandments, if thou wants to fit into thy new jeans.

calliope 11

They say "rain or shine," but I don't think they counted on this. It's been raining for three solid days. The first day people came and braved the elements, thinking it was going to clear up by lunch, by afternoon, by evening. By day two, the crowds had dwindled to a dozen families. Long car trips can make even the most sane father drag his toddlers through the mud. Mothers—either angry or resigned—become walking tissue carriers, sippy-cup bearers, snack providers. Children pull too hard on the marionette strings, lean back too far on the slide, refuse to eat their lunches. Summer trips become death marches. On day three, most of the vendors shut down. The venues closed. Too muddy for jousting. Too wet for theater. Only the beer tent stayed open. Faire workers huddled around tables playing Texas hold 'em, Uno, checkers, chess. Quilts and needlework found their way into laps. Scarves flowed from flashing knitting needles and crochet hooks. Even contraband video games could be heard beeping between the raindrops.

"You know what I feel like?" Abel says, sending one of my backgammon pieces out.

"What?" I ask, staring out at the rain.

"Chocolate chip cookies. Warm from the oven."

"Nuts or no?"

"Nuts," he says, taking a peek at the watch he keeps in his pocket. "And oatmeal."

"That sounds so good," I say, sliding my feet out of my damp sneakers and stretching my legs out along the length of the bench. I roll the dice again, but I can't get the five I need.

"Be right back." Abel pushes himself to standing. He pulls the hood of his blue slicker over his head and walks out into the rain. An identical raincoat lies across the bench near my feet. I found it yesterday morning, hanging on a nail just under the overhang of our front porch, a note in the pocket. *Knew you didn't have one,* it read. *Didn't want you to melt.* I smile as I watch him jump over two puddles before turning the corner and heading toward the arcade.

He had been mad, something I wasn't prepared for. I walked into the tent the first day of the rain, wringing water from my ponytail. I was barely awake, having grabbed a few hours of sleep on the couch after Eliot and his mom dropped me off. I didn't even wake up when Delores got up. Only the sound of the car backing out of the driveway got me off the sofa. Too late for a ride, though. As I pedaled toward the Faire, the first drops came, a light sprinkle at first. By the time I walked into the rib tent, I was soaked. A stripe of brown wound its way up my back where the rear wheel had splashed mud on me.

"It's getting bad out there," I said to Abel's back as I pulled my apron from the table and began tying it around my waist. I set the tubs of sauce near the grill, mildly spicy in front, medium in the middle, and Sweet Jesus at the back. "A real gully washer," I continued. "A real downpour. Noah's bathtub. Raining cats and dogs." Abel finally turned around and looked at me, but he wasn't smiling.

"Cal, hush," he said, staring at me. His blue eyes, normally shining with an untold joke, were flat, empty, hard.

"What are you—" I started, but he just shook his head.

"Why didn't you call?"

"You told me to call if I needed a ride. I didn't need one." I hadn't expected this. Maybe some teasing about how late I got home or why the phone was off.

"Cal," Abel said, taking his cap off and running his free hand over his head before replacing his hat. "You're a smart girl. You had to know I'd be worried."

"We fell asleep." I was aware of how dumb that sounded even as I was saying it. "I was fine."

"I didn't know you were fine. For all I knew—"

"I was fine," I said again, thinking maybe that repetition might be the best strategy.

Abel closed his eyes and made a noise somewhere between a growl and moan. "I didn't know you were fine," he said, opening his eyes again and looking at me. "I . . . was . . . worried."

"I—"

"If you say you were fine one more time, I am going to dump this on your head," he said, pointing to the mild sauce.

"I was going to say I'm sorry," I said.

"Well—"

"Well, what?"

"Say it," he said, holding the sauce in one hand and smiling at me.

"Abel, I mean it. I'm sorry. I should have called." Relief seeped into my brain, my bones, my blood vessels.

"At least next time, leave the ringer on so that I don't have to wake up Eliot's mom," he said. "I felt like a fretful father." He slid the tub of sauce back onto the table.

"I promise," I said, crossing my heart with one finger. We stood grinning at each other until a sound at the front of the tent made us turn.

"Y'all cookin' today?" I turned the dials on the grill as Abel asked the man in the crown about his faraway kingdom. As I draped the first slab of ribs across the hot grate, I couldn't help wondering about another man living in a faraway land. This one not so imaginary. I wondered about a potter in Texas and whether he was ever worried too.

"I *said,* are you in?" Abel asks, shaking off his coat.

"In for what?" I ask.

"Earth to Cal. Man. *Cookies.* Are you in?"

"I am always in for cookies," I say, laughing at the look on his face.

"Well, grab your coat."

"Where did you go?" I ask, pushing my arms into the sleeves and snapping up the front of the too-big raincoat.

Abel sighs. "To get my *truck.*" He points to the parking lot in front of the tent. "Man, a teenage girl in love can be an amazingly distracted creature."

"Yeah, yeah," I say. "What makes you think I was thinking about Eliot?"

"Well, weren't you?" Abel asks, pulling his hood over his head.

"Now I am." I smile at him out from under my hood. We brace ourselves against the rain and make the short sprint to the truck.

I love grocery stores. I love the metallic clang of the grocery carts, the bright yellowy green mounds of bananas, the symmetrical stacks of toilet tissue, the flicker of the fluorescent lights, the hot-pink stickers with TRY ME. I'M CHEAPER! I love the pedestals of samples with broken sugar cookies, paper cups full of lemon pound cake and hunks of cantaloupe and honeydew. I love the fishy-meaty-cheesy smell of the deli, the bright twists of flowers and bob of balloons in the florist, the bad cart that pulls to one side, the quiet jingle of coins being dropped into the registers at the front. I love that no matter where you go, there's a grocery store. The one in Texas may be full of tortillas and avocados, and the one in San Francisco might be full of tahini and lemongrass, while the one in Maine is full of lobster stew and whoopie pies, but there they are. Full of sounds and smells and tastes.

Abel pulls the truck into the parking slot. Raindrops beat against the windshield and rivers of water pour across the lot. "Ready?" he asks, as if we are preparing for a dangerous military assault rather than a sprint to the sidewalk. I nod and we push our doors open and run for it.

He tugs a cart free from the line and starts into the store. "Let's split up," he says. "I actually need to do some real grocery shopping too. You're in charge of the cookie stuff. All we need are chips, nuts, and butter." He steers the cart toward the produce and I scan the signs over the aisles, looking for baking supplies. AISLE 3. CAKE MIXES. PUDDING. SUGAR. FLOUR. BAKING NEEDS.

Clutching chocolate morsels and pecan pieces in one hand, I run my fingers over the boxes of butter and margarine. So many choices. Salted, unsalted, spreadable, Can't Believe It's Not . . .

"Cal, right?" The voice makes me jump. I turn and see Phi

standing, holding a basket in one hand and a bottle of wine in the other. "Long time," he says, and I'm actually thinking, *Not long enough,* but I make myself be nice.

"Phi, right?" I ask, smiling. Well, maybe not too nice.

He chuckles at what he thinks is my joke. As if the possibility of me forgetting his name is ridiculous. He places the basket at his sandaled feet. "Wet out there," he says, plucking a tub of margarine from the stack and nestling it beside a package of Brie and a loaf of sourdough bread. He's not wearing a jacket, and I suspect the damp T-shirt clinging to his chest is no accident. Phi stands looking at me. "I have a daughter about your age." And I'm thinking he has no idea how old I am. "Fifteen, right?"

I nod, a little surprised, and watch him kick at his basket for a moment. "Where is she?" I ask. I shift to let a woman grab a carton of sour cream off the shelf, but don't take my eyes off Phi.

"Last I heard, she and her mother were in Milwaukee with my ex-wife's family."

"When was that?"

"About a year ago."

"When was the last time you saw her?"

"It's been a long time," he says, staring at the yogurts, and by the way he says it, I know it's been a really long time. "So . . ." he says, looking back at me, but the silence continues.

"You're not jousting today?" I ask, to bridge the awkwardness. That's the right button. He begins talking about the proper conditions for jousting, the possibility of injuries, his horse, his lance. About the time he starts talking about his trophies, I see Eliot's mom heading toward us, a bag of Granny Smiths in one hand and a package of Chips Ahoy! in the other. She's walking with her head down, stepping carefully over the lines in the linoleum like I've seen children do. *Step on a crack, break your mother's* . . .

"What?" Phi asks, and I realize I said that out loud.

"I just—" But I stop. Let him think I was bored. I wait until Linda is directly across from us before saying anything. "Hi, Linda," I say, and instantly I regret it because she jumps like she's been shocked. Her eyes are wild and scared and distant as if the sound of my voice had to travel a long way to reach her.

"Cal," she says, and her breath comes out ragged. "This looks bad," she says, finally smiling at me. "It's just been raining and raining and all we have to snack on are carrot sticks and fat-free crackers." She shifts her hand so the cookies are partly hidden behind her. "I feel like a junkie."

"I won't tell," I say. She smiles at me before shifting her gaze to Phi. She doesn't even look at his chest or his arms, only his face.

"You must be Abel," she says, and for a moment I think Phi and I have the same horrified look on our faces. We both shake our heads.

"This is Phi," I say, and try to think of something to explain his presence in front of me in the store. "He's a jouster," is all I can come up with. "This is Linda," I say to Phi, and this time it's easy, "my friend." She shifts the apples and shakes Phi's hand, but instead of looking at him while he grips her hand, she's looking at me.

"We've missed seeing you around," she says, taking her hand back from Phi, and the longing that I've been feeling for the past three days steps up a couple of notches.

"Me too," I say, and I can't help the wobble in my voice.

"You done?" I look around Phi to see Abel heading toward us, his cart loaded up with fruits and vegetables and a couple of loaves of bread. He steers up to the three of us, waggling his eyebrows at the back of Phi's head. Phi turns around mid-waggle and I watch Abel blush a bit, but he recovers quickly. "Phi, what brings you out in this mess?" he asks.

"Just a bit of shopping," he says.

"A bit is right," Abel says, peering into Phi's basket.

"Well, I might be out of here in a few weeks," Phi says, shrugging. "I have something brewing out west." I realize that I am grinning a little too much at that news when I see Linda staring at me.

"I guess I'll—" Linda begins, but I put a hand on her arm, stopping her from backing away.

"This," I say, gesturing at Abel with some flourish, "is Abel."

"Linda," she says, lifting a hand in Abel's direction.

"It's good to talk to you at a reasonable hour," Abel says,

feigning an angry look in my direction. Phi looks a little confused.

"I guess I'll . . . nice meeting . . ." Phi says, and for a moment I feel sorry for him, but then he does this stretching thing over his head before leaving, making all three of us look at him, and any pity disappears. Abel watches him walk away before continuing.

"Is that what y'all serve at that camp of yours?" Abel asks, gesturing toward the package of cookies that Linda is still unsuccessfully trying to hide behind her.

"It's pretty gross," she says, blushing again.

"It's not the choice I would make," Abel says, looking meaningfully at the pile of healthy food in his cart. "I mean, particularly not when you could have homemade Toll House cookies with"—he peers at the bag still in my hand—"pecans."

"That would be heavenly," she says.

"Then it's settled," Abel says, grabbing the morsels and nuts from my hand and dropping them into his cart. I hand him a package of unsalted butter, which he adds to his haul. "You go get that son of yours and meet us at my house in"—he looks at his watch—"forty-two minutes for cookies and coffee and Pictionary."

"Will Eliot's dad . . ." I begin.

"Cal, you let me worry about Eliot's dad. You have cookies to bake," Linda says, smiling at me. "I am going to put these back." She holds the store-bought cookies out in front of her like they smell offensive. She turns to walk back to the other end of the store.

Abel consults his watch again. "Forty-one minutes," he calls out to her, and she shakes the cookies over her head in triumph. As she walks away, she is looking straight forward, not even noticing all the cracks she is stepping on.

"I have two questions," Abel says, letting us in through the back door. We hang our wet coats on hooks by the door and kick our shoes off under the bench. It's the first time I've been inside his house, and I look around as we walk to the kitchen. Bookshelves line most of the walls, even in the hallway. A bright yellow woodstove huddles in one corner, wearing a potted fern for a hat. I run my fingers along the back of the leather sofa as I walk past, letting my hand linger longer than necessary on the fluffy green afghan draped over the back. In the kitchen Abel heaves his plastic bags up onto the island, letting the gallon of milk drop with a thunk beside them. "Okay then, question number one. Pecans. Toasted, or no?"

"Toasted," I say, taking the blue mixing bowl that he hands me. "This is beautiful," I say, using my finger to trace the intricate loops of glaze that circle the inside of the bowl.

"It was my mother's," Abel says, taking eggs from the refrigerator. "It's Polish and supposedly really old." Abel flips on his CD player, letting something slow and sad float out into the kitchen. We work silently, just listening to the music and the rain. Abel slides the first pan of cookies into the oven and we sit on the stools at the island, taking turns pinching knobs of raw dough out of the bowl.

"What's your other question?" I ask, wiping the dampness from my face with a paper towel. I am suddenly aware that Eliot is going to be here at any moment and I have spent the better part of the day trying to run in between raindrops.

"Well, now I have two," Abel says.

"So you said."

"No, I mean two more."

"Shoot," I say, staring out the window at the falling rain.

"Cal," Abel begins, but then he pauses so long that I look at him. He meets my gaze for a moment before looking back down and studying the backs of his hands. "Cal, where's your father?"

"Texas," I say so fast, it comes out clipped and defensive. The timer begins to ping, but neither of us moves. The kitchen feels too hot and too small, and the way we are sitting at the counter suddenly seems too familiar. My tears hit the stone countertop, beading up like the raindrops on the windows.

"Cal, what is it?"

"It's a big state in the south, just below Oklahoma, known for cowboys and oil." I can't keep from smiling. Abel sighs and shakes his head. He walks over and presses the timer, silencing the beeping.

"Okay, this one doesn't count," he says, opening the oven.

"Do you like your cookies soft in the middle or baked all the way?"

"Mushy," I say, wiping my eyes with the paper towel.

"When was the last time you talked to him?" Abel asks, setting the sheet pan on top of the stove and closing the oven.

"Christmastime." I don't look at Abel, afraid of what I might see on his face. "I mean, I tried calling a couple of times this spring, but he wasn't home and then we kept moving." I don't mention that the last time I called, my father's voice poured out of the answering machine, telling me, *We're not home. Please leave a message.* The *we're* made me stop calling. I finally look up at Abel, but he's staring at his hands again.

"It took me a long time to call my father after I left," Abel says, finally looking at me. "I don't know your whole story. I mean, I want to, when you're ready, but listen, Cal . . ." We both can hear tires on the driveway outside, but neither of us moves. "Don't let too much time pass. After a while, I think it's just more time passing, you know? And time. That's something we don't get more of." We hear a knock at the door and Abel pushes himself away from the counter that he has been leaning on. "Go clean yourself up," he says, pointing down the hallway to the back of the house. "The bathroom is on the left, just past the table with the phone on it." He doesn't need to, but he pauses long enough to let this sink in. "I'll get the door." He walks into the living room and toward the back door, but I stop him before he rounds the end of the couch.

"You had a third question," I say, pulling at the elastic that has kept my hair knotted together all day.

"I was going to ask how things were going with Eliot, but the way you flushed when we heard the knock answered that one."

I can hear Abel's laughter and Eliot's deep voice followed by Linda's higher one as I walk toward the bathroom, still yanking at the elastic. I glide my fingertips over the phone as I pass. *Not yet,* I think, *but soon.*

Cal's
Cherry Chocolate Chip
Cookies

1 cup butter

¾ cup brown sugar

¾ cup sugar

1 egg

1 teaspoon vanilla

1½ cups flour

1 teaspoon baking soda

1½ cups oats

1 cup dried cherries

6 ounces chocolate chips

1 cup chopped, toasted pecans (optional)

Cream butter and sugars.

Add egg and vanilla.

Add flour and baking soda, then oats, cherries, pecans, and chips.

Mix gently.

Drop onto lined baking sheet.

Bake at 350 degrees for 10 to 12 minutes.

Yield: 3 dozen

12 eliot

The secret to a good bonfire is lots of fuel oil. I get put in charge of the fire because of my fireworks, but this isn't like The Dad thinking I'm a pyrotechnician or anything. To him my whole firework thing is cute, like I'm twelve and have found myself a little hobby. The only thing is, my little hobby is pretty dangerous, and something like eight hundred pyrotechnicians have been killed in the last fifty years. I read that somewhere. But I get to stack up the wood for Spirit Night, and I stack it up until I can't reach any higher, and then I drain some oil out of the tank at the side of the cafeteria and soak the whole thing in that. It goes up, big and fast and hot. A good fire.

Peto uses his tractor to drag the old bleachers over from the softball field, and some people have guitars, and there are air-popped popcorn and non-fat cookies. A few years ago The Dad tried to invent a no-chocolate s'more, but I mean, c'mon.

"You know what's weird about fires?" Cal says. "My back half is freezing, and my front half feels like it's in a rotisserie oven."

"Your back half feels warm enough to me," I say, my fingers pressed into the back pocket of her jeans.

"No fresh mouth tonight," she says. "Your dad will end up casting out your demons or something."

I nod, laugh a little, my gaze caught up in the fire.

"Hey," she says, "I was teasing. I didn't mean to make fun."

I smile and shake my head. "No, you should make fun. Just look around for a minute." She does, and I do too, trying like I always do to see it from the outside, because I don't want to be sucked in the way The Dad was; I want to guard against that. All the campers are wearing their Sonshine Valley shirts: either the tie-dyed WHAT WOULD JESUS EAT? shirts; or the yellow ones that say GOD DON'T MAKE NO JUNK in Day-Glo bubble letters; or the red ones that just say SONSHINE VALLEY—THE EXPERIENCE OF A LIFELINE, with the same cartoon cross we have painted on the van. The fire pops and cracks, and burned-up bits of plastic bag float in the air above it, from the ceremonial snack-food sacrifice, which this year featured Funyuns. A little while earlier The Dad did a "chalk talk" in which he used a lot of decade-old teen slang ("Let me show you a way to count calories that's really *rad*, kids. . . .") and named vending machines as one of the seven deadly sins. I told Cal that they could get rid of sloth to make room for vending machines, since no one talked about that one much anymore. Two guitars play "Kumbaya," and people sing along, and The Dad keeps announcing what the next verse will be (*"We'll eat right, my Lord, we'll eat right . . ."*), and I watch him, how much energy he pours into it, telling myself that he really has helped people . . . the office wall has a bulletin board full of people and their before/after pictures. This one kid, the same one I noticed the first morning, stands looking into the fire, praying with his hands clasped together, like a drawing of someone praying, and I notice in the glint of the fire that he's crying, the tears shining down his pink cheeks.

Cal notices too, pushes me slightly with her own hand in my back pocket. "That kid over there, what's with him?"

"I don't know, he was like that the first day too."

She shakes her head, leans into me. "You know, for all the cheering and clapping, they all seem so sad. Like the singing and stuff is just this plastic cover over everything."

"Yeah." I watch him, the way he lets the tip of a stick burn in the fire, then holds it up to blow it out. Even from here I can see how much he is sweating, and he looks like one of the biggest kids we've ever had here. Just moving to sit on a log seems to leave him fighting for a breath. I let my hand move up Cal's back, feeling the little knobs of her spine, then back down.

"Is it always like this?"

"Sometimes better, sometimes worse. One time was cool, this guy from Zambia came to speak. You know, in Africa?"

She smirks. "Thank you, Alex Trebek."

I give her a quick kiss. The Dad calls out to tell us the next verse (*"Calories count, my Lord, calories count . . ."*). "Anyway, smarty, the Zambian guy told us that where he lives, the heart isn't the big symbolic thing; it's the liver. So you have to ask Jesus to come into your liver. You ask God to cleanse your liver of sin."

She smiles big. "I love that."

I nod. "I kept wondering if on Valentine's Day they give each other liver-shaped boxes of candy."

"Eliot," she whispers, then hugs my arm so I feel her breast pressed against me, "I love you with all my liver." Then she throws back her head and laughs, making me laugh.

"Cal," I say, "my liver yearns for you."

"Actually, that's kind of gross. Like a doctor might tell you that you have a yearning in your liver, you need surgery right away."

I laugh again and notice then that The Dad is watching us. He's on the other side of the bonfire, and he has his hand on the shoulder of the crying kid, who is using his smoldering stick to melt the tip of his sneaker. The Dad is frowning, at me, at us, at my arm around Cal. I think he wanted her here to get saved, not to be my date. And as much as I want to just turn my back and not care and just hang on to Cal, I do care, on some level. I want him to like her, to like *us*. I want him to laugh the way he used to, before his laugh became one that he practiced for TV shows. And Mom? She is nowhere around, and I haven't seen her all night, just her shadow on the drapes of their cabin, moving back and forth, then fading away when the light finally went out.

✦ ✦ ✦

All during the drive to Carolina Beach, we take turns arguing about which radio station to listen to, and every time a song comes on that has the word *heart* in it, Cal replaces it with the word *liver* and cracks herself up. I watch her and realize that about ninety percent of the songs on the radio have the word *heart* in them. The three of us are crowded into the front seat of Mom's Honda, Cal in the middle. It feels warmer and warmer, the farther south and east we drive, the sun high above us in a cloudless sky.

I've never seen Mom like this. She stops for gas and asks us if we're hungry, and while Cal and I wash the windows and check the air in the tires, Mom goes into the convenience mart and comes back out with a bagful of stuff—honey buns and pecan rolls and biscotti and little white doughnuts and little chocolate doughnuts, plus every packaged snack food you could think of. She slides into the car, wearing shorts and flip-flops and a T-shirt from some band she used to listen to. She tosses the heavy bag into Cal's lap and slips her large coffee into the cup holder.

"You kids knock yourselves out," she says. She looks at the bag as if seeing it for the first time. It looks like it could be a bag of laundry, and she laughs. "I mean it," she says. "Rot your teeth, ruin your appetite. Put yourself in a diabetic coma."

"The three cornerstones of healthy living," Cal says, and Mom laughs way more than she probably should. Cal even looks at me, and I just shrug. I try to stay in it and have fun, and I am having fun, Cal's hair tickling my face in the wind, and her bare thigh pressed next to me, and the music and all the jokes about stupid billboards and road signs. But I also keep thinking about The Dad, and how he must have felt when he woke up and got the note from Mom, which, she told me, just said that she was taking a little vacation for the day to Carolina Beach and would be back by dark. I think of him moving through the cafeteria at breakfast, trying to think of what to say to the girls, blushing as he talks to them. He always does. And I think how he always tells me to make it back in one piece when I take the van out, and I know he's worried about us.

Cal bites into a honey bun, then gives me a bite of it too and wipes the corner of my mouth with her finger. "How come every packaged snack food has two names?" she says. "I mean, look at this, Ding Dongs, Ho Hos, Devil Dogs, Ring Dings . . ."

"What about Zingers?" I ask her.

"It's still two syllables. They all end up with either two words or two syllables."

Mom nods, looking at the pile in Cal's lap, then back at the road. A sign tells us we are forty-three miles from Carolina Beach. "You're right," she says. "Yodels, Sno Balls, Twinkies. That's just weird."

"Not so weird," I say, watching the highway move under us. "They all use the sounds of children's rhymes, the same rhythms and patterns. Twin-kie, Ring Ding, we all fall down . . . right? Little nursery rhymes."

Cal looks at me, smirking. "And why is that, Professor Eliot?"

I puff on a pretend pipe. "Well, isn't that obvious? It gives snack cakes the illusion of childhood innocence and fun. They aren't guilty of anything; they are just little and cute and naive. They would never do something as terrible as clog up our arteries or rot our teeth or make us fat."

"You sound just like—" Mom starts to say, then stops herself. "Just like a very odd kid." She looks at me and winks, but it's too late, and an awkward silence settles over us until Cal finally breaks it.

"I'm really sorry, Professor," she says, "but how do you explain *these*?" She holds up one of the cellophane-wrapped packages. "*Swiss Cake Rolls*. That doesn't rhyme; it's not cute; it's not childlike. And this is one of our most-respected snack foods, is it not? How is that, Professor? Hmmm?" She nudges my thigh with her own.

"Well," I say, "isn't it obvious?"

"I can't wait to hear this," Mom says, leaning into Cal.

"We trust the Swiss for their ability to engineer things, to build with precision," I say.

Cal looks at me. "We do?"

"Do I even have to mention Swiss watches? Swiss Army knives? Swiss cheese? If anyone can build a non-threatening, non-lethal snack cake, it's the Swiss. They're neutral, we can trust them not to attack us with trans-fatty acids and sugar. I think you would feel differently if they were German Cake Rolls. North Korean Cake Rolls. I bet you wouldn't eat them."

"I bet I would," Cal says, and takes a big bite out of one. "You have a very strange son," she says to Mom.

Mom shrugs, smiles. "I did the best I could," she says. "Twenty more miles." Her hands knead the steering wheel. "Is anything looking familiar?"

A few miles later, it does start to look familiar, only smaller. We cross the bridge and drive past the Totem Inn roadside zoo, where I used to laugh because the monkeys would carry peanuts with their tails, where they had on display a two-headed goat in a bottle of formaldehyde, and Mom wouldn't let me see it, and I finally saw it because I lied and said I had to go to the bathroom. We pass Tex & Shirley's Pancake House and the 3-D Chowbox and the place with no name on the outside where The Dad would stand at the counter and eat raw oysters while Mom made faces. She gets more and more quiet the farther we drive, and I guess I do too, looking around at everything I haven't seen in seven years, while Cal gives my hand slow squeezes. We drive right through Carolina Beach, and most of the same places are still there: the T-shirt shops with pirate flags and Confederate flags and Boogie boards and beer bongs hanging from ropes around the outside, and places that carry seashells you would never find here in a million years, and all the bars with neon signs, and the telephone pole outside the

7-Eleven where I used to chain up my bike, and Playland with the merry-go-round that for some reason has tigers and camels but no horses. The Ferris wheel is there, and the roller coaster, and they look like someone left them in the dryer too long and shrank them down. I remember how afraid I was of them then, how my parents made a big deal of it the first time I went on alone, but now I can see that they're—just harmless little-kid rides, circling around the same way for the last thirty years or so. Maybe it's that way with everything, all of it smaller when you come back and look at it later. I wonder how any of this might be smaller for Mom, or maybe it's bigger to her because of the ways that she has gotten small, the ways she's shrunk into herself the last few years.

When we get to the street where we used to live, Mom turns on the left blinker, slows, then hits the gas and keeps driving straight.

"Such a nice day," she says. "Why don't we hit the beach before anything else?"

We both nod and say OK, and it's three blocks before she remembers to turn off the blinker. It's cloudy, threatening rain, so there is hardly anyone on the beach, and parking is easy. Cal stands up out of the car and stretches, wearing her cutoffs and sneakers with no laces, and she tells me that if she has to eat another snack food, she is going to turn into an eight-year-old.

"They sell hot dogs up on the pier," I tell her.

She nods. "There's one up there with my name on it."

"That's a weird thing to name a hot dog," I say, and then for a second I can't breathe as Cal strips off her T-shirt and underneath she's wearing a green bikini top, her skin so pale and smooth, so full of soft curves.

She smirks. "Your turn to strip, my turn to stare," she says. I laugh and do exactly that, while Mom hauls a folding chair and a small cooler out of the trunk. We walk along the sandy pavement, me between them, bumping shoulders.

"I don't know, Eliot," Mom says, as if she were picking up some conversation we'd just been having. "What do you think happened, between here and there?"

Cal skips off ahead after giving my hand another squeeze. "You two reminisce," she says. "I'm looking for sharks' teeth."

I shake my head. "I don't know," I say.

"I'm forty-three years old," she says, as if this is another part of a conversation that fits together in her head, as if she's connecting dots. "You're too young to know what I'm talking about," she says, then laughs. "What I'm *not* talking about, I guess."

I see Cal up ahead, running down to the edge of the breakers and just looking out at them, the wind lifting her hair. "It's like we left something behind," I say to Mom, and try not to think about The Dad and the fact that we have left him behind. "It's like there is something that we used to be, and we just forgot to pack it when we moved, and if we went back to the house it would still be there in the corner of the attic."

She stops at the edge of the sand and looks at me. "I take it back. You aren't too young." She takes a deep breath, lets it out. "I want you to know, Eliot . . . I believe in God just as much as he does. I mean, not that it's a contest, but we have very different ideas. I don't think you seek out God directly, or else He would just come down and visit us once in a while. I think He wants us to seek him out through other people, through being in love with the world. He's in the ocean, He's in a bagful of snacks and the way you end up laughing about them. He's in the laughing. Does that make sense?"

I nod. "He's not in a T-shirt. He's not in a medallion you wear around your neck."

"He might be in that bottle cap Cal wears, but yeah, you're right. You do understand." She shakes her head, then pushes her hair back. "Promise me one thing. Promise me you will never shut your life down or shut your heart off in the name of obligation, okay? I mean it. Make your life big, and it will fill up with the right things, I promise you."

I nod. "It would almost be easy not to go back, you know?"

"Yeah, easier, I think." She shifts the cooler to her other hand.

"What's going to happen?"

She hesitates. "I don't want you to worry, not ever. But I don't know what's going to happen. I will tell you this, Eliot. Whatever that thing is that got left behind in the attic? I need to find it and take it with me, or I'm going to make myself crazy looking."

I nod, though I don't really know what she means. Cal is up to her thighs in the water, the edges of her cutoffs darker blue where they're wet, her hands up as though trying to push back the cold of the surf.

"Go on," Mom says. "Go be with her."

I fall into the day with Cal, and by the time a couple of hours have passed, it's like I've forgotten about everything Mom said, or at least have been able to put it aside for now. She goes for a long, long walk down the beach, until she is a dot that disappears into the mist and then a while later reappears, growing bigger. While she's gone we lie on the blanket and kiss, and Cal rests with her head on my stomach, looking up at the clouds, and for a time we watch this guy behind us who is flying this big stunt kite, holding a controller in each hand, and when the wind gusts the kite cuts hard to one side or the other and he gets lifted into the air by the force of it.

"Does this feel like home?" Cal asks.

"Yeah, it does." My fingers play with her hair and make little circles on the top of her shoulder.

"Which part the most?" she says. "The water? The pier? The gritty hot dogs?"

"No," I say. "*This*. You right here, with me, beside me. That feels like home."

She grows still, quiet for a long stretch of time before whispering to me. "That is the nicest thing anyone has ever said to me."

"That?" I say. "That's nothing. I have a lot more to say that's nicer than that. Just stick around and see."

Then she is quiet a different way, and turns her head away from me. "Cal?"

She gives her head a little shake, and I lean up on my elbow to see her, a single tear slipping down her face, toward her ear. "Cal, what's wrong? Tell me."

When she finally speaks, her voice sounds wet and shaky. "Delores is going to leave, to follow that dumb-ass Phi. He's galloping off or something. She's going."

"Well, no, I mean—"

"Eliot, I'm her daughter. I'm fifteen. I have to go with her."

I just stare at her, shake my head, and stare some more. "But you don't want to," I say. "I don't see why—"

"If they let fifteen-year-olds do what they want to, there would be like maybe three people in any given sophomore class."

I shake my head again, my stomach collapsing in on itself, my heart hammering the inside of my chest. "Cal, we can think of something. There has to be some way. Make her stay. Make yourself stay."

"My best plan so far is to wait three years. You want to wait that long, Eliot?"

"I will."

"No, you won't. If I go, I won't ever see you again."

"Stop. Don't. There has to be something—there *has* to be."

"There has to be, and there isn't," she says, turning away again. And the silence we fall into is as big as the ocean.

✦ ✦ ✦

178

That night we are in the backseat so we can stretch out to sleep and, I think, so Mom can have time to herself in the front seat, where she listens to oldies stations on the radio, a few of her CDs, and hums along to herself. Cal sleeps, leaning against my shoulder, breathing in a deep way that is almost but not quite snoring. My fingers stroke her hair, my arm asleep behind her neck. Mom turns up the volume slightly for a song she seems to know really well, because she sings this time instead of just humming. The song is a quiet sad one, and the singer keeps talking about her lonely heart breaking, and I smile a little, remembering that morning. Was it only twelve hours before when we were laughing and eating and heading off into the sun? Can one day hold so much change? I want to think about these things like they are problems in philosophy or chemistry, little intellectual puzzles to ponder over, but they are questions sent up by my heart, not my brain, and none of the questions have any answers.

"Cal," I whisper into her sleep, "if you go, you know what? You'll break my liver." I want to pretend that it's a joke, that she will wake up and laugh with me, throwing her head back the way she did last night, but this time the words are true . . . she will break my liver, break my heart, kill everything alive inside me.

13 calliope

Maybe it was the surf music that we listened to on the way back from the beach. Not actual surf, like waves crashing and loons crying, but Jack Johnson meets that Hawaiian guy whose name I can't say or even spell. Lots of guitar and ukulele and words about love and the rhythms of life. It was the perfect score for the journey back. The trip wasn't a happy let's-go-to-the-beach kind of trip. I mean, there were moments when I was as happy as I can ever remember being, but those were matched by moments so sad I could almost feel my heart breaking. Delores would probably say something about perspective, like how I can't possibly understand love when I'm only fifteen. But the thing is I think I can understand love precisely for that reason. And, I'm not just talking about Eliot and me but about Eliot's parents and Delores and Phi and Abel and nobody and my dad and whoever the other part of "we" is on his answering machine. I think that maybe when it comes to love, Eliot and I are the smartest people I know. It's like we both got to the top of our diving boards and just looked at each other and jumped. And we just keep watching each other, enjoying the fall. While everyone else around us is still either stuck up on their boards or frantically trying to brace themselves for the impact. Or they're like Delores. They're just climbing back down the ladder, deciding that the most they want to do is wade into the water. Get their feet wet.

Eliot thought I was asleep and I guess at points in the trip I was, but I heard him say that my leaving would break his liver. I almost started crying again right there in the backseat, but I couldn't because then he might know how scared I was too. So I pulled within myself so far that all I could hear was his breathing and my breathing and then just breathing. Somewhere between the beach and the mountains, I realized something. I realized that if I lost Eliot, I might never let myself jump off the board again.

The sunlight is bright through the windows and I stretch my arms overhead. It was late by the time Eliot dropped me off and my eyes feel itchy from lack of sleep. Linda let him take the van to bring me home. "Only to Cal's and back," I heard her say before she kissed him on the cheek and told him to be careful. He followed her instructions in theory. I mean, the dirt road we pulled off on wasn't actually on the way, but it wasn't out of the way either. Eliot pulled an old camp blanket out from under the backseat and laid it out in what he kept calling "the way back." It was nice to be completely alone, but scary too. I knew that some things were changing between us, big things. We kissed for a while, Eliot half on top of me. Then he leaned up on one elbow and looked down at me as he traced my jaw and my lips with his fingertips. I closed my eyes, relaxing under his touch, feeling his fingers on my neck and then across my shoulders and then along my side, trailing all the way down to my hip bone where the side of my bikini peeked up from my shorts. My breathing changed with his as he slid his fingers across my stomach and up to my chest. Suddenly Eliot stopped and rolled back, groaning.

"What is it?" I asked, sitting up.

"You make it hard to stop," he said, leaning his head back against the spare tire.

"Do I?" I smiled at him in the dark.

"Cal, I just want to take it slow. Make sure it's right."

"With God?" I placed my hand on the center of his chest, feeling the strong, fast beat of his heart.

"With us," he said. "I need this to be right."

"You need us making out to be right? I think if we have questions, there's probably a book or something." I slid my hand down his chest to his stomach, but he caught it before I could go any lower and secretly I was grateful. I wasn't sure I was ready for that. Eliot leaned forward again so that our faces were only a few inches apart.

"Here's the thing, Cal. And I need you to really hear me. No Miss Smarty-pants, okay?" I nodded, not taking my eyes off his. "This. Us. This is the real deal. If we take care of this, it could be the forever kind of deal." He looked at me for a minute before leaning back against the tire and closing his eyes. "I know. You're going to say we're fifteen. You're going to tell me I don't know what I'm saying. That we don't know each other well enough."

"Eliot?" I said, laying my head on his chest. He put his arm around me, pulling me into him. "I wasn't going to say any of that at all."

The bedroom is starting to get hot and I force myself out of remembering last night and toward the kitchen. "I should get my hair cut," I say to myself, shoving my hair up into the Red Sox cap that Abel let me borrow.

"Your hair is beautiful just the way it is." The voice makes me jump. I thought I was alone. Delores is sitting at the table, peeling an orange, trying to work it off in one long strip. While she eats the segments, she always rebuilds the orange with just the peel, so that from the outside it looks whole, but it's completely empty.

"What are you doing here?" I ask, pulling the milk from the refrigerator. I look over at her working at the peel, an inch at a time, rotating the orange in her hands as she peels the narrow strip away from the segments.

She looks up at me, letting go of the peel for a moment to take a sip of her coffee. For an instant I think she is going to answer the larger question that I've just asked. *What are you doing here?* As in, what are you doing moving us every few months? As in, what are you doing purging nearly everything we own every quarter? As in, what are you doing dragging me away from the one place that I have called home in the last four years to follow some superficial, self-involved poser all the way across the country? But all she says is, "I live here," before returning to her orange.

I shake oat flakes into a bowl and cover them with too much milk. Delores likes just a splash, but I like to drown my cereal. I push through the Brie and half-empty wine bottles in the refrigerator, trying to find the berries that Eliot and I picked. "Where are the blueberries?" I ask, more of the refrigerator than of Delores.

"Phi ate them," Delores says.

"Of course he did," I say, pushing the refrigerator door closed. I grab my bowl and sit on one of the stools at the counter, then stir my cereal slowly with my spoon, watching the flakes turn into mush.

"Not enough sleep last night?" Delores asks. She wasn't even here when I got in, so how would she know? She's been spending more and more time with Phi, apparently happier staying in his tent or in the back of his van than here. "You've been spending a lot of time with that Eliot," she says. And she says *that Eliot* the way someone might say *that criminal* or *that trash*.

"His name's just Eliot," I say, still stirring.

"Okay, grouchy," she says, picking up the orange again and twisting it to find the place that she left off. "You've been spending a lot of time with *Just Eliot*." Again I think how would she know? Every once in a while Delores tries for the whole I-think-it's-about-time-we-had-a-mother-to-daughter-talk talk. It always comes out forced and scripted like one of those bad after-school specials. *Mommy, I'm Dancing with the Devil* or *Mommy and Daddy Can't Live Together Anymore, But We Still Love You*. Today's programming seems to indicate that our special is *My Daughter Might Be Having a Relationship That I Should Talk to Her About Even Though I Haven't Given Her the Time of Day Since I Am Too Busy with My Own Life*. That seems a little long, though.

I keep stirring my cereal, aware that by this point it has gone beyond nicely soft and is clearly headed for Nastyville. I watch Delores's fingers as they pry the peel from the orange segments, sending up puffs of orange oil into the air.

"Where'd you get that?" she asks, nodding at the blue bowl in the center of the table, holding the eight or so remaining oranges.

"Abel," I say, picking up a spoonful of my cereal and letting it dribble back into the bowl. Abel gave me his mother's bowl on the day that I will always remember as Cookie Day. I even suggested that June 9 should always be Cookie Day, making everyone laugh.

"It's"—and I wait for *nice, beautiful, amazing*—"big," she finishes.

"It's beautiful," I say, a little too loud.

"If you like that sort of thing."

"What sort of thing is that?" I ask. Delores looks up at me and all I can think is, *Here we go.* . . . It's as if I can see the her that lives inside. The real her. She is standing right behind her eyes and is staring directly out at me, and I wait for it. I wait for her to say anything at all, but before she does, something in her eyes shifts and I watch her retreat again. She walks back and sits down, looking away from me.

"I don't think I want to talk to you anymore," Delores says, placing her orange on the table and unfolding herself from her chair. I don't look up at her when she passes me to place her mug in the kitchen sink. "You let me know when you are ready to have a grown-up conversation," she says, pulling her jacket from the peg beside the door. I keep stirring my cereal, watching the slow whirlpool of flakes and milk until I hear the sound of her car pulling out of the driveway. For some reason, I can't stop crying as I slide the rest of the orange into a Ziploc. Somehow, during our orange-scented conversation, Delores pulled the peel too hard and it broke. I can't help thinking that now there's no way to build any kind of orange, even one with nothing inside.

+ + +

I wonder if it's possible to feel nostalgic at fifteen, especially about something you've only known for a few weeks. Downtown is full today. Summer season is in full swing. Families pushing kids in strollers and couples holding hands clog the sidewalks. I let myself get carried along in the tide of people walking past the shops, past the kite shop, past the candy store. The couple in front of me slows down in front of the clock shop, pointing at the Elvis clock in the window ticking off the seconds with his hips. The clocks are set for time zones all over the world. A conch shell is set for Eastern Time, North Carolina time, Abel time, Eliot time. A Felix the Cat clock with eyes that look from side to side in time with the seconds is set for Central Time, Texas time. A clock in the shape of the lighthouse at Quoddy Head on the coast of Maine is inexplicably set to Mountain Time. Its candy-cane stripes spiral down the sides, falling off into the ceramic rocks holding back the waves. A girl in a grass skirt hulas rhythmically as she ticks off Pacific Time. I suddenly panic when I realize I'm not sure whether New Mexico is in the Mountain Time Zone or Pacific. Two hours, three hours. How far away will I be? I want to ask someone, anyone, but everyone keeps walking by like the world isn't imploding. Like in less than a month, my life isn't going to shift back into the nothingness that I can now barely remember.

I will myself away from the window, sliding into the space behind a man carrying an enormous box almost too big for his arms to reach around. He is bent back under the weight of it, shifting his balance so he won't fall forward as he steps off the curb to cross the street. I follow his steps, sideways past a fallen ice-cream cone. He slows down when he reaches the other side, and I watch him work his foot forward, searching for the curb. He can't see anything past the top of the box, past his own arms. He steps up on the curb and continues forward, trusting that people will move out of his way, that the sidewalk won't suddenly buckle or change directions. I wonder if his eyes are closed. If he's just walking forward blindly. I wonder if he worries at all that he might trip and fall or drop his box, but then I see her. In front of him on the right is a woman holding the door open, talking to him, guiding him forward with her voice. She's been there the whole time, walking in front of him, warning him of the ice-cream cone. Telling him to be careful of the uneven bricks in the intersection. I stop and lean against the arched brick entryway to a shop, watching as she talks him up and over the steps and into the shop. She places her hand on his lower back as he passes, following him through the doorway and inside.

Santa Fe in twenty-seven days. I can still hear the laughter, the excitement in Delores's voice when she told me we were leaving. *I thought we'd be here at least until fall,* I said, feeling the floor tilt under me. *Plans change,* she told me, as if that was reason enough. I lean my cheek against the bricks, feeling the coolness against my hot skin. It's been four days now, but it's not getting better like before. The scrambled feeling in my stomach isn't going away like it has in the past. There's a clawing inside of me. A desperate feeling of being trapped. I keep praying, hoping to find a door, but the walls are smooth. I shift my hands along them, but there's no secret button, no hidden handle. In twenty-seven days, I will be going away from here. Away from North Carolina. Away from Abel. Away from Eliot, and there's nothing I can do about it.

The spiraling light catches my eye, this time not just red like the lighthouse clock, but red and blue. I watch as the lines travel downward into the silvery base, only to show up again at the top. Falling again and again. I take a deep breath and turn and pull on the door handle behind me, the only one that actually is there when I feel for it.

"Cut it all off," I say, lowering myself into the chair. I hold Abel's hat on my lap, rolling the bill of it as I've seen Abel do with his hat when he's nervous.

"You sure?" He spins me until I am facing the mirror. I don't look up at myself, afraid of what I might see.

"All of it." I twist the cap hard, like I'm trying to wring something out of it. Behind me, the chairs are starting to fill with the lunchtime crowd. The little-off-the-top crowd. The just-clean-it-up-a-bit crowd. I imagine on most days they're talking, about the weather, about deer season, about whether the Panthers are going to do anything this year, but today they're quiet. Their heads are bent low over *Guns & Ammo* and *Ducks Unlimited*, trying to act like an article on hollow-point bullets or a new way of building a hunting blind is the most interesting thing in the world. But I think the most interesting thing in their world today is me. Because today I'm here for a haircut.

"There's a beauty shop down the block," the barber says, but I shake my head before he can finish. I feel bad for him. I'm sure he thinks I'm crazy. Maybe he has images of my mother coming in here and threatening him with his own scissors, but that's a laugh. It might be weeks before Delores even notices.

I keep my head bent as he drapes the cape around me. The white fabric settles slowly, shifting across my bare legs with a rustling sound. I hear him lift the metal plunger from the glass cylinder on the counter, extracting one of his combs and flicking it to remove the blue water.

"Scissors, okay?" he asks, tapping the pair on the counter with his fingers. "My clippers will make a mess of all of those curls." I keep my head lowered as he lifts the back of my hair and drapes a towel over my shoulders. "Last chance," he says, gathering my hair into a ponytail at the back of my neck. I feel him flip the ends in and out of a rubber band. "Just in case you want to take it with you," he says, pulling at the ponytail to slide the band snug against the base of my head. "All right, then," he says, more to himself than to me.

"All right," I whisper, and I make myself look into the mirror, where I see half a dozen pairs of eyes staring back at me. I stare into my own eyes as I feel the gentle tug of his scissors. He has to work at it to make it all the way through. I close my eyes as I hear the blades of the scissors meet and I suddenly feel an incredible weightlessness. I actually hear one of the men gasp as he pulls the bundle of hair free.

"Do you want it?" he asks, and I open my eyes to see him holding my hair like a fisherman might hold his catch of the day. I shake my head and suddenly I am laughing, imagining tourists lining up to get their pictures taken with my hair. The men waiting begin talking softly, but the volume builds quickly. *Show's over.*

Abel is bent over the roses, clipping the heads off the dead ones. I watch as he carefully steps between the bushes, pushing the branches aside to keep them from snagging his clothes. He leaves a trail of pink and yellow puffs in his path. I haven't told him we're leaving. I begged Delores to let me do it, knowing she'd botch it and end up hurting him without even realizing it. She tells me she has a good heart, tells me that it's what's inside that matters, but I don't think that's right. No one can read the contents of your heart. It's what you say, how you act that matters. I take a deep breath and walk toward the backyard.

I step along the stone pavers that lead into the garden. I think of Linda walking in the grocery store, careful of each step. *Step on a crack, break your mother's . . .* but it's not funny when you're mad at your mother. "You have a thing against flowers?" I ask, balancing on the last square.

"Just the pretty ones," Abel says, without turning around. He keeps clipping, working with his back to me. "It's not the flowers in specific. Really it's a problem with beauty in general. It just doesn't impress me."

"Really. So, you're in favor of ugly?" I ask.

"I wouldn't say 'in favor.'" Abel stands up and puts his free hand on his lower back. "It's more the uniqueness of ugly that I appreciate. I mean, you've seen one rose, you've seen them all, but man, show me an ugly flower and you're really showing me something." I go to tuck my hair behind my ears, but there's nothing there to tuck. Abel turns and looks at me.

"I cut it," I say, shoving my hands into the pockets of my shorts and looking at the ground.

"Yourself?"

"The barber."

"Cal, what's going on?" Abel steps toward me so that I can see his sandaled feet.

"We're leaving," I say, and I try not to cry. Black sandals. Pink roses. Green grass.

"You cut your hair because you're leaving?"

"Yes. Well, no. It's . . ." Silver shears. Brown dirt. Yellow lilies. ". . . complicated."

"God, Cal," he says. I look up at him, but he's staring beyond me. "Did you tell her? I mean, did you tell her you don't want to go?"

"Yeah."

"She didn't listen." Abel looks at me, rubbing at the back of his neck with his hand.

"Delores doesn't change her mind once it's made up."

"Santa Fe?" I nod at him and he nods too.

"God, Cal. I wish—"

"Me too," I say, looking past him at the willow tree. Its branches hang low over the garden, trailing along the ground at points.

"I need you to promise me something," Abel says so softly that I have to look at him to make sure he has actually spoken.

"Okay."

"I mean really promise." I nod this time.

"I need you to promise me that you won't hurt yourself again."

"My hair?" I ask, touching the curls on the side of my head. "Abel, it was just a haircut." But, even as I say it, I realize that we both know the truth. "I promise," I whisper.

Abel smiles with his lips closed, looking past my shoulder again, then back at me. "I feel like I'm supposed to say something smart now. Something wise. Like how it's all for the best or how it'll be okay, but those things aren't smart or wise. They're just things to say."

"There's nothing to say. I mean, nothing that is going to make it okay."

"I guess not," he says, opening and closing his shears.

"Better get back to destroying some more beauty," I say, smiling at him.

"Seems like enough beauty's been destroyed for one day," he says, turning to walk back into the garden. I watch him pause over a shriveled bloom for a moment before clicking the shears closed.

I start to walk toward the stairs up to the apartment, but I stop and walk back to the edge of the garden. "Is it okay if I use the phone?" I ask. Abel turns and nods at me. "I've been meaning to make a phone call for a long time." I start across the driveway and don't even need to look back to know that Abel is staring at me as I step though the back door and into the house.

I pedal slowly, just watching the spokes as they spin around the axle, away from me and then back again. Like hands on a clock, spinning too quickly, wasting time. The breeze feels strange on my head. The helmet feels too big, sloppy without all the hair to hold it on. I push harder on the pedals to keep my speed even as I climb the hill to the camp. Eliot said between two and four he's usually at the pool, lifeguarding. I circle the back of the cafeteria, afraid I might see his father there. I saw the looks he kept giving us at the bonfire, felt his disapproval almost hotter than the flames. I roll slowly toward the pool, hearing the splashing of water and the screeches of young girls through the trees. Eliot sits in the guard chair, hunched forward, his elbows on his knees as he watches the swimmers pass through the water beneath him. I lean my bike against the fence and unclasp my helmet. I pull it off my head, running my hand across what's left of my hair. It's even curlier than before, short spirals, pulling tight against my head. I see a flash out of the corner of my eyes and realize that it is Eliot's glasses, catching the sun as he turns and sees me. I raise my hand and give a quick wave. He waves back, but it's slow, deliberate. I point over to the picnic tables and he nods before looking back toward the water, then he blows his whistle, and the swimmers leave the pool.

I lie on my back on top of one of the tables, watching the branches move in the breeze above me. I must have drifted off because the next thing I am aware of is someone kissing me. I open my eyes and shift my head back to look up. Eliot is staring down at me, smiling.

"You cut your hair," he says, reaching his fingers out to brush the hair just above my ear.

"You hate it," I say, watching his eyes.

"No," he says, still smiling at me. He bends down and kisses the side of my neck. "Easier access," he says, his breath warm against my throat.

"Eliot."

"Yes?" he whispers into my neck.

"We have an audience." He sits back and sees the half-dozen girls watching us. I sit up and the girls hurry away, giggling behind their towels.

"I missed you," he says.

"We just saw each other like fifteen hours ago."

"So, you didn't miss me?" he asks, kissing my shoulder.

"A little," I say, shifting so that I am facing him.

"Well, I was going to ask you something, but I'm not sure I'm going to now."

"What?" I ask, leaning forward to rest my head on his shoulder, so warm from the sun.

"It's kind of silly," he says, and I notice that even the side of his neck turns red as he blushes.

"What?"

"See, there's this end-of-camp dance, and I was wondering if you might want to—"

"Yes," I say, smiling up at him. "I want to." We sit for a few moments, just watching the kids chase the soccer ball in the far field.

"I kind of have something else to ask you," Eliot says, and I notice that he's blushing again. I nod, looking up at him. "The thing is, Peto kinda found my chemical stash for my fireworks and he threatened to tell my dad about it. And, I thought about just ditching the stuff because I already have all my fireworks built for the end of camp, but they kinda cost a lot of money and I kinda need—"

"You need somewhere to keep them." He nods at me. I think for a moment about the apartment, but it's way too small to keep anything hidden. "We could keep them at the restaurant."

"You don't think Abel will mind?"

"I'm thinking we don't tell Abel. I mean, they're harmless, right?"

"Totally," Eliot says, smiling at me.

"Any more questions?" I ask, poking him gently in the ribs.

"Do you still love me any?" Eliot asks, putting his hand over mine.

"A little."

"A little?" he asks, pulling away from me.

"A lot."

"How much?" he asks.

"More than chocolate chip cookies."

"Mmm," he says, kissing my shoulder.

"More than walking on the beach." Eliot kisses me on the neck.

"More than . . ." I pause, turning to look at him.

"More than?" he asks, kissing my lips.

I turn toward him. "Anything."

14 eliot

The day of the dance, two days before the end of camp, I wake up and the whole camp has this weird buzz, this strange vibe where it's like the air just feels different and you know something is up. I pull on shorts and a T-shirt and head outside, where Peto is walking around the grass on this side of the lake, wearing his blue coveralls and frowning.

"That kid," he says. "He is missing."

"What kid?" I ask, though right away I have a pretty good idea.

"His name is Riggs," Peto says, in an accent I can never quite nail down. "They tell me so I can call his name."

My first question is why Peto is looking for a missing kid by wandering around in the short grass by the lake. This is a *really* fat kid, I want to tell him, not an Easter egg. I also wonder why he's carrying his orange Weed Eater, like it's some kind of fat-kid detector, but with the way Peto has been poking around my fireworks shed lately, the less said the better, I think.

Riggs, of course, is the name of the kid I noticed from the first day, who spent most of his first week here alternately crying, praying, sitting out the activities, and openly eating contraband food. I mean, one day he sat out the tug-of-war (which The Dad renamed Sin and Redemption) and sat on the bleachers eating out of a one-pound bag of M&M's. The Dad just watched him, hands on his hips, too shocked to do anything right then, I think. That kid might as well have been sitting there using heroin. Twice he has had his locker and bed searched, and nothing turned up, and still the next day he was back at it with Raisinets or Twix or, once, a bottle of Yoo-Hoo. I think he might be magic, but right now he's just gone.

Summer-camp tragedies seem so commonplace, it's like everyone expects them. A kid drowns ten feet from the dock, or falls into a ravine during a day hike, or hangs himself in the showers, or wanders off and is found in the woods a week later, suffering from hypothermia. I mean, it's almost like newspapers have these stories on file, and they just whip them out when the time comes, change the name of the camp and the kid, good to go. And something about the way it's so expected makes it seem like it could never happen to us in a million years, but then I think, *what if?* What if that's Sonshine Valley mentioned in all those stories, what if it's our driveway full of satellite news vans? What if something really is wrong?

I wander away from Peto, who continues to look behind trees and under benches, like he thinks the kid is invisible or maybe just playing hide-and-seek, and I head toward the cafeteria, which seems to be the center of things. From a distance I can see The Dad passing out sheets of paper, and then the other campers take off in pairs.

At least for me this is some distraction from thinking about Cal's hair. I mean, a possible dead kid versus a serious haircut, and I start to feel kinda small-minded, but still. I felt sad, like her hair had gone missing too, like I was expecting it to come back any minute. And she kept telling me that it *would* come back, in about ten months or so. I didn't let on. I said that it looked really great, and how I always got a real haircut at the start of summer, and how pretty she was, and how it showed off her eyes even better, and I made her smile. That's part of the deal, with something like that. Like, a girl could wear a porcupine on her head and a burlap sack for a dress, and she'd say, *Do you like it?* and if you're the guy you have to say, *Yeah, it looks great, wow.* But that's not really me, and usually I just say if I don't like something. But this was different. It seemed like she was sad, too, that her hair was gone. In ways that hair *was* her, the way she gathered it up in her hands all the time, bundles of it all coppery and thick, the way it lifted in the wind when we rode the big slide, the way it moved when she did or fell down around me like a curtain when we kissed. Put it this way—it's the first thing you notice about her. But she had given it up, one

pass with the scissors, she said, and the barber threw it away. I
kept feeling almost like her hair had been *taken* from her, that
thought kept pushing in, and then I realized—she had taken it
from herself, deprived herself of something she loved so much.
And I started wondering why that might be, how she could be
that mad at herself, and I knew in about three seconds it was
because she was leaving. She told me once that moving so often
meant you never got attached to anything you really liked—a
photo album, a favorite book, even a sweatshirt—all of these
she'd been made to leave behind at one time or another. Now
she was leaving me, leaving Abel, and I could almost see it.
Like, why take *anything* you love? Leave it all behind, even if it's
part of you.

I find The Dad on the loading dock of the cafeteria, and he
has a map of the entire camp and his bullhorn, which has never
really worked right.

"No sign?" I say.

He shakes his head.

"Where's Mom?"

"Out looking, with everyone else. Or who knows? Where
have you been?"

"I was sleeping, Dad. I didn't realize."

"Another late night?" He keeps his eyes not on me but on his
map, circling parts of it with a carpenter's pencil.

"You could've woken me up," I tell him, remembering when
I was eight and he would rouse me in the dark to head to the

beach because the blues were running. "Tell me where to look."

He skims over the map and circles another part of it with his red pencil, but I can tell the way by he does it that there's no system involved, like he's just trying to use a map and pencil and bullhorn to make himself feel like things are under control. His hands shake as he holds the map. He's panicking. "Wherever," he finally says. "Try the chapel, try the mini golf. . . ." He waves his hand, looks at me. He's sweating, even though it's only nine in the morning. "Anything," he says.

I try to focus on finding Riggs, try not to picture him dead or hurt, try not to wonder about his name, which sounds more like a verb than a name. Most of all I try not to think about Cal going away from me. First her hair, then her, leaving me in pieces. And leaving me in pieces. Yeah, clever, if only it weren't totally true. I close my eyes, feeling the gravel under my feet, and then open them and I'm standing at the old putter shack near the mini golf, where she touched my arm for the first time when they came out here to ask about the cabins. I say, "Riggs" a few times, feeling mostly stupid. I mean, if he *wants* to be gone, hidden away (and after watching him this week, I'm thinking that's probably right), it's not like someone is going to say his name and he's going to pop up and say, "Yes?" But I say it, anyway, because in movies that's how they search for people, and I poke my head inside the windmill house, and then into the pump house for the pool, and I try not to think that this will still be me in a month, only I will be wandering around saying Cal's name, never thinking to look in Santa Fe, so far from here. I call his name a final time, into the empty shed, where only a few dust motes move around in the light.

There is new buzzing around the loading dock, and I jog back over to see. The Dad is running his hand through his hair, then tugging on his ear until it reddens. I have yet to see Mom today, but I figure she's still out looking for Riggs. The new buzz turns out to be a note, found not on Riggs's pillow, but *inside* it, between the pillow and the pillowcase. I change those every other day, so I guess Riggs figured someone would find it. The Dad holds the note, reading it several times, and I can see it's written on the back of a Daily Menu Planner in purple glitter pen.

"Is that like a suicide note?" one of the campers asks. She pushes her hair back behind her ears, her pale face blushing pink.

"No," The Dad says, almost angrily. "It doesn't make sense."

"Well, yeah," another kid says. "He might not exactly be a straight thinker right at the present." He wipes the sweat from his face with the bottom of his T-shirt and, with the half-dozen other campers crowded around, considers the idea that a suicide note wouldn't necessarily be clear. I can tell from their faces that after a couple weeks of salads, baked fish, sermons, forced fun, homesickness, and sing-alongs, this is the first real excitement they've had.

"What do you think, Eliot?" The Dad says, and hands me the wrinkled note.

"Well, right off, I think no one serious about doing themselves harm would say so in purple glitter pen."

"I can do without the smart-aleckness," he says.

I sigh. "Just trying to lighten things up a little," I tell him, cutting my eyes at the campers who surround us, before I start to read:

To Who It May Concern:
This is not the Way. Narrow is the Way does not mean youre
body. Original sin was pride and that's this whole place, we
even sang a song about it. Jesus walked on the water and
healed the ill and that seems to be not noticed around here.
I am not taking my body to heaven and niether are you.

R. W.

"What do you think?" The Dad says.

"I think he's not really on board with the program."

"Eliot . . ."

"Dad, I don't think it's a suicide note. I don't think he even ran away. I think he ran *off* for a while, like he needed a break. I mean, where would he go?"

"That last line scares me a little," he says. I read it again and nod and don't say that it scares me too. He looks so worried, so old all of a sudden, and I try not to think that this is the second bad note he's had in a week. For a minute I'm mad at Mom, at both of us, for taking off on him, leaving him with stuff like this.

"We'll find him by lunch," I say.

The strange part of all this is that the end-of-camp dance is still on for that night, two days away from the actual end. As I walk past, I can see through the windows of the cafeteria all the chairs and tables folded away, another group of campers on stepladders and milk crates streaming gold and white crepe paper everywhere, hanging paper fish and sea horses and lanterns, and I can smell turkey hot dogs cooking, and Peto has installed the disco lights that The Dad bought at RadioShack a few years ago, and there's a long table set up with an empty punch bowl sitting on it.

Cal took us to Goodwill a day earlier to buy clothes for the dance and said we weren't allowed to look at what the other was buying, it would be bad luck. I wanted to say that I didn't see how our luck could get much worse, but I could tell the way she was acting that she just wanted to have fun for a night, for a couple of days, and forget the idea that she was leaving. I tried to forget it too, I swear, but it was like this plastic film over everything, closing off everything we said and did. She'd worn my favorite pair of jeans and her purple shoes, and I watched her walk away from me, into the back part of the Goodwill, the absence of her hair almost a thing itself. I made my way to the men's department, past the sad and broken toasters, the lidless Crock-Pots, the dirty Sit 'N Spins, the binful of albums by people like Perry Como and Mr. Spock and that guy who sells denture adhesive on TV. I found a baby-blue tuxedo jacket with dark blue trim all over it and this huge dark blue bow tie stuffed into the inside pocket, plus a ruffled shirt with tiny black buttons. Pretty dorky. There were no pants with it, either, but it didn't matter. I knew Cal just wanted us to be all funky and look a little weirded out, and the jacket and tie were only five bucks. They just rolled it up and stuck it into a paper bag, then she made me wait outside while she paid for hers.

I head for the upper lake, where the paddleboats are, figuring no one's going to look up here because of the steep climb up the hill. There's a small beach of trucked-in sand, and the first thing I see is Mom sitting near the dock in her workout clothes, hugging her knees to herself. She's crying, silently, wiping the tears away with the back of her hand, careful not to scratch herself with her ring.

"Mom?" I say, walking up beside her. "Are you okay?"

She smiles a little bit and pats the sand for me to sit. When I do, she says, "You know, Eliot, your powers of observation astound me." She points out into the lake; I shield my eyes against the sun, and there he is. Riggs, floating with the breeze on one of the paddleboats, a yellow one, just slowly twisting, an orange life preserver hanging limp around his neck, looking puny against his bulk. He's reading a book, a Bible, I think, from the black cover, and eating some kind of snack food from a cellophane wrapper.

"Ding Dongs, Ho Hos, Yodels," Mom says, and we both smile, both relieved.

"Have you talked to him?"

"Of course. He makes a lot of sense too."

I nod. "He doesn't look like he makes a lot of sense."

She sighs. "Just ask him."

"Ask him what?" I pick up a stick and make little circles in the sand, trying not to think too much about the night Cal and I paddled out into the lake and let the moon wash over us.

"Ask."

I stand up and cup my hands around my mouth. "Hey, Riggs," I shout, though he's close enough I really don't have to, "what are you doing out there? You need to come back in."

"Jesus walked on the water," he says. "Jesus calmed the waves."

I look down. "Mom . . ."

"Keep talking to him."

"Well," I shout to him, "don't try to walk on the water, okay?"

He licks the wrapper of his snack food. "I'm not *stupid*," he says.

"I know you aren't, but what are you doing out there? Come on in, okay?"

"Jesus called the Pharisees 'whitewashed tombs' . . . said they were clean and white on the outside, black and foul on the inside. That's *this* place." He puts his wrapper on the empty seat and the wind lifts it out into the middle of the lake, where it floats and spins.

"What do you mean?"

"I mean, what else is a tomb? It's solid, rock, perfectly built. You don't see too many flabby tombs, Eliot."

I'm a little startled to hear him use my name, even though we've all been wearing HI MY NAME IS _____ tags all week. He keeps talking.

"If I'm to carry the good news to all corners of the world, I need to look like the world, not better than the world. The world is fat, Eliot, most are, and who needs the Gospel most? The kids here, all of them lonely and broken and hating themselves. They need *the word*, not jumping jacks." He pulls a pack of peanut M&M's from his pocket and starts eating.

I sit down again. "Okay," I say to Mom, "he's crazy."

"He's a little messed up." She starts crying again, the tears splashing as she blinks. "But what are we? We have a poster of Jesus wearing boxing gloves, Eliot. Jesus is buff; Jesus is *sexy*. Sex sells, Jesus sells, so it had to happen sometime, right? I'm glad I could help it along." She says this like she is sick of herself, and maybe she is.

"It's not you; it's Dad. And he does help people."

"A pretty weird way to help people. Mostly it's business, Eliot. I know, I pretty much run the business part. Your dad goes out and sells it, same as he ever has. This is just a bigger swimming pool. One full of drowning people."

I nod. "What's going to happen?" That seems to be the question, and I can ask it of almost everything in my life.

"I don't know." She shakes her head. "Tell him to come on in. He'll listen to you."

"Hey, *Riggs*," I shout. "Come on in, man. Listen . . . I'll call your folks, and you can leave here early. Today."

He looks up, still chewing. "Really?"

"Really. No tricks. You don't have to stay."

Riggs nods once, and by now I can hear some of the others making their way up the hill. But mostly I hear Mom, still sitting beside me, quietly whispering to herself, over and over, what I just said to Riggs: *"You don't have to stay . . . you don't have to stay . . . you don't have to stay . . ."*

The DJ this year plays real music (last year's played only music by Christian singing groups, all of which were pictured on the CD covers wearing sweaters), and the kids go a little nuts, in a good way. Girls dancing in tight circles, the boys letting themselves be dragged out with almost no fight, groups of kids still doing the Macarena and the Electric Slide, all of them whooping and shouting and laughing, dancing until the room feels warm and moist as a greenhouse. I think that for some of them this may be the first time in their lives that they aren't pinned to the wall by self-consciousness, wriggling under their own awkwardness. Tonight, this one night, *they* are the cool kids, and they are busting it out, drinking the punch, eating the turkey dogs, and then dancing and dancing and dancing. It has been only three hours since Riggs's parents showed up in a rusted pickup truck, and he squeezed in the middle between them, headed home, but the kids seem to have forgotten already.

My own self-consciousness is a little more out there than usual tonight, because it turns out that Cal can *really* dance. I mean, I can hold my own, and I don't do the usual guy thing of just tilting side-to-side like Frankenstein or else waiting for the slow dances so that all you have to do is hold on and revolve. No, I can dance okay, but Cal is amazing, and she looks amazing. She dances with me and with Mom and with some of the kids, and Mom seems to be dancing with everyone but The Dad, who is mostly not there—off, I guess, in his office. Cal wears the dress she bought at Goodwill, so pale pink it looks like the color could just fall off if you weren't careful with it, and the fabric seems to float around her, chiffon, she called it, and it's strapless, her breasts rounded and perfect and freckled. It's an old dress, like something from a black-and-white movie, and with her short hair and wearing makeup, she looks that way to me, like some beautiful actress from an old movie you'd run across on TV at two in the morning. Only this would be some special kind of black-and-white movie, where she is the only thing in it that's in color, her hair, her green eyes, her pale pink skin and dress held up against the gray world behind her.

God, I love her.

During one of the slow ones, I pull her close to me, feeling warm and flushed, the layers of her dress pressed against my thighs, my fingers moving across the skin of her back, right where her dress stops. Breathing moves between us in a back-and-forth, and I realize that I'm making it do that, want to do that, to breathe in as she breathes out, drawing her breath into me. My hand slides along the taper of her waist, over the curve of her hip, my fingers slowly memorizing her, learning her like Braille. Earlier that day I'd gone into town and stopped at Terry's Florist to buy her a corsage, knowing this was likely to be the closest either of us ever got to a prom, and now the sweetness of the roses and baby's breath seems to rise up from her pores, to wrap around me. One of the roses she'd tugged free of the corsage so that she could pin it to the lapel of my tuxedo jacket, but the smell makes me sad too, somehow, or maybe it's the smell of the clothes themselves, that attic smell, the odor of something put away and forgotten.

"I love you," I whisper.

"I love you too," she says, the little dots of light spilling over us, tiny moons. I open my mouth to say something else, and she shakes her head.

"Leave it at that," she says. "Anything else will just be sad." And she tucks her head into the hollow of my shoulder, pressing against me.

We move slowly together, and I kiss her shoulder, her ear. "I'll wait," I whisper. "I'll wait until you can make it back here, make it back to me."

She shakes her head, won't look up at me. "No," she says finally, "you won't."

The music ends, the lights come up, and the DJ announces a Hula-Hoop contest. Finally she pulls back enough to look at me. "See?" she says. "Sad. You should listen to me sometime."

She walks outside and I follow her, find her sitting on the bench looking out at the same single goose who seems to always be awake, the insomniac goose, we've taken to calling her. Cal is barefoot, has danced barefoot all night, her shoes left somewhere inside.

"One day, and my hair's longer already," she says as I walk up behind her. "See, I told you, I'm a hair-growing machine."

"I was wondering when they were going to perfect that."

She shakes her head. "No, not perfect, not by a long shot."

"Yes," I tell her. "You are. For me."

She smiles. "I like the qualifier. Okay, yes, I am perfect for you."

I sit on the bench beside her.

"I finally talked to my dad," she says. "The DJ talking about a blast from the past? He's got nothing."

The day before, while we moved my chemicals into the basement of the Cloven Hoof, she told me that she planned to call him that night, since Abel would be out and she would have the house and the phone to herself. But then she didn't want to talk about it anymore, and I had never seen her that nervous. At first I thought it was the chemicals making her nervous, and I guess it was partly that. I mean, about twenty times she asked it if could start a fire, and twenty times I told her no, they couldn't. What I didn't say was that they could sure as hell accelerate a fire, thinking it was better for her not to know that.

"What did he say?" I slip my hand into hers.

"He talked about golf. His new set of irons, how much Jennie was improving, his handicap. I mean, *golf*? My handicap was I had no idea I had a father who played golf, and no idea who Jennie was. Jennie." She shakes her head.

"So who is she?"

"My stepmother. What do you call that, when you have a relative you don't even know about?"

I shrug. "A gift from God?"

She laughs. "Mr. Cynical. I told him we were moving. Again. Still. Always." She squeezes my hand tight.

"What did he say?"

"He's mad. He doesn't like it. He thinks I need a real home."

"There?"

"No. I don't think I'm ready to move to Texas and caddy. I don't think I'm ready to move to Texas period. I need to blonde-up a little first. And you know, I wanted to say to him, 'If you don't like it, why don't you make her stop?' I mean, he must have some . . . whatever you call it."

"Parental rights?"

"You are the cutest dictionary I ever met," she says, and kisses me.

"So," I say, "if you want to say that to him, then why don't you? Tell him to make it stop."

"I can't. Delores . . ."

"You *can*. Cal, Delores doesn't—"

"Eliot, stop. I can't."

I nod and tip my head back on the bench. An hour from now I'm supposed to end the dance by shooting off fireworks, and I have set up in the mortar tubes by the lake ten charges of Peacock Plumes, Whistling Flowers, Creepers, and Whirlwinds; and I don't care much about any of it. All of it seems like noise and false light, and all I want for tonight is the quiet, the black and gray of a summer night, and a girl in a pink dress, beside me forever.

I was swirling water into coffee mugs, scrubbing at them in an attempt to get rid of the brown circles that ringed the insides, when I saw the three beach balls, one right after the next. I dried the first mug, pressing into the cup the nubby terry-cloth towel with a drawing of Santa Claus on it. It was really early, way too early for me to be up, but then I'm not that good at sleeping in even the best of times. Only the vaguest sense of dawn was beginning to touch the tips of the trees, turning the leaves at the very top a watery pink. I'd already cleaned the bathroom, tub and all, and was tackling the kitchen, and there they were . . . one, two, three beach balls. Instead of really noticing them, I just kept swirling the soapy water in the mugs, stopping every swirl or two to sniff the corsage that rested on the windowsill. After more than a week, the smell was probably more in my memory than in the shriveling flowers, but I kept leaning over it, eyes closed, breathing in the faint scent of flowers and smoke.

The first ball was blue-and-white striped, about the size of a good jack-o'-lantern. It bumped once between the buildings, catching some air before sinking and drifting behind Abel's fence. The second was one of the ones that you can buy at Wal-Mart for eighty-eight cents, the yellow ones with the smiley faces on them. Its face kept rolling around it and I wondered if it got dizzy, spinning that way. The last one was the smallest, purple with black letters that I knew said *Four Winds Renaissance Faire* even though I couldn't read it from the window.

I looked down at the pink ribbons, twisting out from under the roses of my corsage. One of the ribbons had a black smudge on it to match the black handprint on my dress. Eliot let me stand on the far side of the lake with him while he set off the fireworks, telling me to keep back as he moved between the lengths of PVC pipe pushed down into the ground to hold each bundle. He told me the names of each as he moved, checking fuses and changing their angles. Names of exotic birds and rare flowers floated toward me in the darkness. "This one's Peacock's Plume," he said, bending low over the first tube. "Flaming Orchid," he said, adjusting the angle on a big one. "Russian Rainbow, Sea Anemone, Starry Night." He kept walking, his voice growing fainter as he moved away from me. "Red Dragon, Picasso's Revenge . . ."

"You've named them all?" I asked, watching him bend over the last tube.

"Yeah," he said, barely audible in the dark.

"How about that one?" I asked as he pointed the last firework into the sky above the lake.

"This one? This one's my favorite." He straightened up and walked back toward where I stood, just under one of the pine trees that ringed the lake.

"Well, does it have a name?" I asked as he slid his arms around me.

"It does," he said, leaning forward to kiss me.

"Are you going to tell me?" I asked, leaning against him.

"Cal," he said into my neck.

"Yes?" I asked.

"No, that's its name. Cal."

We stood and held each other in the dark, watching as the kids poured out of the dance and onto the docks and the grass on the other side of the lake. The lights went out in the cafeteria and I saw Linda step out of the darkness and toward the water. She lifted her hand in our direction, smiling like she had been all evening.

"You ready?" Eliot asked, before kissing me one last time. I nodded into his chest. I watched as he moved between the sunken pipes just as before, but this time he carried a smoldering stick in his hand, which he used to light each fuse. I kept my ears covered, hearing only the faintest whistle as each one lifted from the ground and gained altitude. A dull thud was followed by a spray of color that lit up the clearing and made the kids on the other side of the lake cheer. One by one he sent them up, and we watched as each one exploded into a dazzling light before leaving only the faintest trail of smoke to let us know it had actually lived for a moment, bright and wild in the dark sky. I watched as he bent over the last one, my firework, and I fought the urge to tell him not to, to just leave it. I held my breath as he touched the glowing ember to the fuse and watched as the flame slowly crawled up the length of it and into the body of the firework. With a flash of light it launched into the sky, whizzing overhead in front of the moon and out over the lake. I heard the pop of the containment tube bursting from the pressure of the flame. I watched as one by one fountains of colors burst from the tube, first red, then white, then green, before the tube began to fall back to earth, gaining speed as gravity pulled at it. It disappeared behind the trees, making me lose sight of it, but I swear I felt its impact throughout my body as it hit the ground.

The lawn chair is the thing that makes me stop doing the dishes, the thing that makes me look harder at the bit of street I can see from the kitchen window. It isn't until I pick up the second coffee mug, the one with JESUS IS RAD in red block letters on it, the one Eliot gave me, that I see the chair. Then, right after, the top of a barbecue grill, its red metal top swirling past, like a cherry floating in a limeade. That is followed quickly by another chair just like the first, a kid's wading pool, an umbrella spinning in circles, and a garden bench. For some reason it is the garden bench that makes me slide my feet into my flip-flops and walk outside. Maybe it is the solidity of it, the metal-and-wood heaviness of it that makes me decide to walk around Abel's house and toward the street.

"What's going on?" I ask. Abel is standing barefoot in his front yard, watching the water rush down the street in front of us. Only his stone wall has kept the water from flooding his yard as it has the houses on either side of us.

"Water main is my best guess," he says, watching an unmanned canoe floating past. The sirens in the distance grow louder by the moment. "Somewhere up the street," he says.

"What should we do?" I ask, stepping up to the wall and staring down. About two feet of crystal clear water is rushing past now, making it look as if Abel's house is standing in the middle of a river.

"Not much we can do, I guess," he says, running a hand across his bare head. "The wall seems to be keeping the water out of here. At least for now." Someone shouts into a bullhorn, but it's too far away to hear the words. "Want to go look-ee-loo with me?"

"Want to what?" I ask, staring at him.

"You know, want to go up the street and stand around and say things like 'So, what's the situation?' and 'What are y'all doin'?'"

"Well, yeah," I say. "I'm sure they love that."

"I've got a couple pairs of rubber boots in the garage. They might be too big, but at least they'll keep your feet dry." I follow him to the garage, where he hands me a pair of pink boots with daisies painted all over them.

"Don't ask," he says, and by his tone I know he really means *Go ahead and ask, just not right now.* We walk out of the driveway and away from the flood, circling around until we can see the rolling lights of the emergency vehicles bouncing off the houses at the end of the street. "I was afraid of that," Abel says so softly that I'm almost not sure he has spoken at all. I watch his mouth move a bit, trying to find words, but he doesn't say anything more.

"What?" I ask, touching his arm. "What were you afraid of?"

"Look," he says. He points to the street sign on the corner.

"Ridgecrest," I say, reading aloud. I keep walking forward, watching as the water reaches higher and higher on my boots the farther we go down the street. "Abel, I'm sorry, I don't mean to be obtuse. . . ."

"The restaurant backs up against Ridgecrest," he says, walking faster. I have to hurry to catch up with him.

"God, Abel, I didn't think—" and I didn't. I was too busy daydreaming and watching the water to think about anything. Abel looks over at me, seeing the wetness in my eyes.

"Let's just wait and see," he says, touching my shoulder. "No sense crying over spilled . . . well, no sense crying." I follow him all the way up to Main Street, where half a dozen firemen are standing around in hip waders. Two of them are leaning against the back of the kite shop smoking cigarettes, which seems wrong in so many ways. I hang back as Abel walks up to the one closest to us.

"Hey, Pudge," Abel says, and the nickname suits him.

"Abel," Pudge says, taking a drag off his cigarette. "Terrible thing, man."

"Can you shut it off?" Abel asks, watching the burbling hole that continues to spill forth thousands of gallons of water per second.

"No can do," Pudge answers, letting smoke drift out of his mouth and through his mustache. I am reminded of the smoke in the sky after the fireworks and turn away to watch the kids starting to play around the edges of the flood pool. "It's one of them thirty-six inchers. We just have to wait for them to divert the flow up at the plant."

"How long will that take?" Abel asks. He looks back at me for a moment and flashes me a slight smile. A kind of don't-be-scared-everything-will-be-fine smile, but I think it's as much for his own benefit as mine.

"Don't know," Pudge says, dropping his cigarette butt into the water pooling around his feet. I watch as the nub floats past Abel and out into the street to join the other debris being carried downtown and downstream. "They might've already done it, but that don't mean the water'll stop right away." He reaches down to scratch at himself, forgetting that he's wearing the waders. His fingers scrabble around on his stomach for a moment as if they are tiny animals, burrowing and searching before returning to his face, hands once again.

"How long before the pipe clears after they shut it down?" Abel asks.

"Hour. Maybe two," Pudge says, extracting another cigarette from his shirt pocket. "Make yourselves comfortable. Might be a while." Abel sloshes back to where I'm standing, right in the middle of the road, and stands beside me, not quite touching my shoulder with his. We watch silently from our position right on the yellow arrow indicating that you can only turn left from this lane. A banner across the street informs me that NORTH CAROLINA IS FOR LOVERS, but I thought that was Virginia. Two boys row down Main Street in an inflatable raft, splashing water at each other with their plastic oars. The barber who cut my hair, the florist who made my corsage, and the sad woman with the dress shop all join us, standing slightly apart from us. Funeral distance, I think, watching them gather around. And it feels like that, like a funeral. But one with kids laughing and kicking water at each other and a woman in purple boots passing out doughnuts and paper cups of coffee. One with firemen smoking and scratching themselves and with a father and his toddler chasing a beach ball along the curb. And with one more thing that makes me think this whole business might be a dream. At some point while I am watching the people gather around us, Abel starts laughing.

* * *

"Tough break," Phi says, kicking at the drywall with the toe of his cowboy boot. He manages to put a hole right through the soft plaster and looks around quickly to see if anyone saw him do it. When his eyes meet mine he shrugs slightly, then bends down to wipe at the toe of his boot. He walks back toward the kitchen, retrieving his cup of coffee from the counter. Since he's been here, I have watched him drink coffee, flirt with the Red Cross lady, eat a chocolate-glazed doughnut, and now kick a hole in the wall.

The restaurant is filled with a dozen or more people trying to dry as much as they can as quickly as they can. I can hear Abel's voice drift over the crowd every so often as he tells people where to put things and whether to throw things out or not. I keep pressing the beach towel into the floor with my hands, having abandoned the mop once I got most of the water up. Abel told me that he is luckier than some with his wooden floor. He might get some warping and buckling, but those with carpet will have to pull it out altogether and start again.

"So, then he asks me if I know Jesus." Delores's voice drifts out of the kitchen, where she is helping some people go through the pantry.

"I hear he's crazy," a male voice answers. "I mean, let's-make-some-toxic-Kool-Aid crazy."

"Maybe," Delores answers. "He's definitely fanatical enough. He wouldn't let me leave until I told him that I'd been saved.

Then he started in about Cal, telling me that it was my responsibility as her mother to ensure that she had a rightful place in heaven." I keep pressing at the towel, watching my wet handprints appear in the striped terry cloth.

"Seems like Cal's pretty tight with his son." The other voice has dropped in volume, but not enough.

Delores doesn't change her voice at all. "It's just a summer thing. You know how it is when you're fifteen." I hear Delores laughing and sit up on my heels in time to see Phi wrap his arm around her shoulder.

"Am I just a summer thing?" Phi asks, pulling Delores into him.

"Well, you know," she says, smiling up at him, "like mother, like daughter." I can feel a hard pressure behind my eyes as I listen. I want to walk into the kitchen and tell her that I am not like her. That I never want to be like her. That Eliot is more than a summer thing. Instead I go back to pushing at the towel, pressing my hands against the floor harder and harder, until my wrists are sore.

"You're gonna put a hole in the floor if you push any harder." I sit back on my heels and look at Eliot standing over me. He crouches down in front of me and touches my cheek. "You okay?" he asks. I nod and begin bundling the towel together. I start to stand up, but Eliot puts his fingers on my arm. "It's going to be okay. I mean, Abel has insurance and . . ." But I start shaking my head. "Then what is it?"

"Nothing," I say, not looking at him.

"Something."

"Just the same old stuff."

"Your mom?" he asks, and I nod. "You don't have to let her push your buttons, you know."

"But she's so good at it." I smile up at him. "I mean, I think she might have her doctorate in button pushing."

"Ph.D. or M.D.?"

"Definitely Ph.D.," I say, standing up. "It's really more of an art than a science." Eliot takes the towel from me and tosses it into the basket that holds all the other towels I've gone through. "I mean, some of it's the same, but she changes it all the time."

"Kind of like the Vietcong." I look at him sideways and squinch my eyes at him. "She continually changes the torture," he says, "so you don't lose consciousness."

"Eliot, you are one weird guy," I say, giving him a poke in the ribs.

"So long as I'm your guy," he says. I smile and nod at him.

"Shall we?" I ask, pointing toward the stack of folded beach towels on one of the tables.

"Nothing would please me more, Miss Calliope," Eliot says, pulling two towels off the stack. He hands the one with blue and green stripes to me, keeping the one with pink palm trees for himself. Kneeling side by side, we begin pressing the towels into the floor, watching our handprints as they form one on top of the other.

* * *

"He said it was an act of God," Abel says, rubbing at the back of his neck. "Apparently you can't insure yourself against God." Abel and Linda are sitting on the top step of the porch while Eliot and I are taking turns kicking water at each other in the street. Most of the water has been gone for a while, but pockets of it still remain in low parts of the street and against the sides of buildings.

"Will they cover *anything*?" Linda asks.

"All the equipment is covered under a separate policy, so that's taken care of, but the structural stuff isn't." Eliot follows me over to the porch, and we both sit on the bottom step so that our shoulders are touching.

"Well, the main thing is going to be getting that drywall out of there so you can let the studs dry out," Linda says. Eliot and I both turn and look at her. "Get some big fans in there and crank up the heat. The longer the framing soaks in the water, the worse it's going to be." She gets quiet when she notices all of us staring at her.

"Go on," Abel says.

Linda blushes a little, but continues. "Well, once everything dries out, it's a pretty simple fix to bring in some new drywall and nail it up, do a quick tape job, a couple of coats of paint. You know . . ." She trails off, watching the stream of people walking past, gazing into the open shops along the way.

"No, I don't really know, but you seem to," Abel says.

"Mom did all the renovating at the camp," Eliot says.

"With your help." She pokes Eliot's back with the tip of her sneaker.

"I was the trained monkey." He makes a face at me. "Mom's the one with the engineering degree."

"Engineering?" Abel asks, leaning back against the porch railing.

"Yeah, I was one of those nerds with a slide rule and pocket protector in college. I was going to build bridges the rest of my life."

"Really?" Abel says, waggling his eyebrows at us.

"Also," Eliot says, waggling his eyebrows back at Abel, "she put herself through school working as a carpenter."

"Well . . ." Abel begins, but then he stops and stares out into the street, watching the people stroll by.

"I'd be happy to help," Linda says quietly. "I mean, if you want me to."

"The thing is," Abel says softly, "I don't know what kind of money I would have to pay you."

"Tell you what," Linda says, placing her hand on Abel's arm. "You pay me in food until we figure it all out. Okay?" And Abel seems to like the way she says *we* as much as I do because he smiles for the first time all evening. Eliot cuts his eyes at me.

"I wonder if this is what Noah felt like," Abel says, staring at the cars parked along the curb on the far side of the street. All of the cars are half clean, bisected horizontally as if some misguided graffiti artist had used water instead of paint to create his work. Abel sighs, shaking his head. "'Course, Noah had a little bit of warning, I suppose."

"Noah didn't have friends like you do," I say.

"No, I guess he didn't," Abel says, but he sounds far away when he says it. Then he turns to me and smiles. "Sorry. Too much Old Testament when I was young, I suppose."

"Abel, I don't think this means the world's ending," I say, smiling back at him.

"I don't think of Noah's flood that way," Linda says. Her voice is quiet in the growing darkness. "Sure, God wiped out a lot of stuff when He made it rain for all those days and nights, but I think it was more about cleaning the slate than about destroying things."

"It's like He just shook up the whole world like a snow globe and then set it back down, gave Noah and his family a new start," Abel says.

"I never thought of it that way," I say, tucking my hand into Eliot's. He laces his fingers through mine and squeezes my hand three times. *I love you too,* I squeeze back.

"I think the flood was less about endings," Linda says into the night, "and more about beginnings."

eliot 16

Mom and I make our third trip to Lowe's this week, loading up
the back of the van with drywall and spackle and tape. Plus,
after the walls came down, Mom was all over Abel because his
place wasn't insulated. ("Why don't you just turn on the oven and
burn all your money?" she asked him.) And he had only one
smoke detector in the whole place, which wasn't wired in the
right way, so we bought those too, the back of the van full of
boxes and pink rolls. She was going a little nuts, and it seemed
to be that way since that night on the porch when she asked
Abel to pay her in food, which he'd been doing. We spent most
of our time away from the camp now, eating meals that Cal and
Abel cooked for us either at his house or at the Cloven Hoof.
To pay for materials, Abel keeps having what he calls "sidewalk
sales," which means he cooks ribs and barbecue inside, then
sells it outside, in Styrofoam containers. We do our best to keep
dust and paint out of the barbecue sauce. Mom has been on

Abel about his health too, explaining to him one day that pickles don't count as vegetables if they're the only ones you eat and, two days ago, convincing him to go on a "jog" with her through downtown. They took off together, laughing, while Cal and I watched them, Mom in her running shorts and top, and Abel in Chuck Taylors and an old pair of gym shorts from maybe 1975, faded red with white piping around them. That and a T-shirt that said HAPPINESS IS LAKE ERIE! They ran about eight feet, and Abel stopped, pretending to be out of breath, and asked if that was enough for today. Nice, really nice, to see Mom laughing again, spilling out of her like it's been pent up for years.

But then sometimes we are all in the restaurant, me and Cal and Mom and Abel, and maybe Pudge drops in, or a bunch of other friends that Abel has—he's one of those people, he seems to know everyone in town—and we are having the most fun I can remember having since I was little, listening to oldies on the radio, laughing and working sometimes until way after dark, and yet I feel terrible, like one whole corner of me is always reserved for terrible, no matter how much fun the rest of me is having. And it *is* fun. I mean, even last week, when we were just getting started, we were knocking down the bad Sheetrock with sledgehammers, and it was late, and we fell into this game where every time someone knocked a good chunk out, the rest of us had to stop and say what the hole looked like ("Nevada . . . a goat's head . . . a paper airplane"), and then these old songs would come on the radio, stuff I never heard of, and Mom and Abel would sing, badly, as loud as they could.

But I would think about us, me and Mom and The Dad, stuck out there at the camp, living here seven years and not knowing *anyone* in the town, and how much we'd missed out on, but now it feels like Mom and I have decided to join the town, and Dad is all by himself there, still stuck, missing out on all of us. At the end of last week Mom moved into one of the other cabins, and the sad part was it didn't change anything that much, make much difference. And as much as I wanted to ask her what was going on, it didn't seem really that necessary, because anyone with eyes could see what was going on. She took off her ring to work on the drywall, and I haven't seen it since, and twice at breakfast I found the newspaper folded to the "Apts Unfurn." section of the classifieds.

The morning after the campers left, I skipped out on work at the restaurant and drove out to find The Dad, and when I pulled into the gravel lot I put on the brake and just sat there looking at the place like I hadn't seen it in a long time. And actually, I hadn't, not *really* seen it. I thought about the morning that the geese hunters came, how bad that was, but somehow this is almost worse—all the quiet, all the emptiness. Like that was killing, but this was death.

"Hey, son," he said when I found him, "what's shakin'?" I didn't have to look for him too hard. He was at his desk, as always, typing at the computer with a ledger book open on his lap.

"Not too much," I said. I knew if I told him about the flood he would talk about God using punishment to tap on our shoulders or something like that, and so I just said nothing. Anything else I could think to tell him about—Cal, Abel, Mom, the work on the restaurant—all of it seemed like stuff he wouldn't want to hear, or care about hearing. We stayed like that, in silence, listening to the whir of the cooling fan on his computer.

"Hey, you know what? You are here at a momentous time. Just made a big decision." He slapped shut the ledger book.

"What's that?"

"No more camps," he said. "Not after this year. And hey, great fireworks. You really sent us out with a bang."

I tried to laugh at his usual joke, the same one he made every summer. "Why no more camps?" I said, though I figured it was because of Mom.

"Because of simple economics," he said. "We just don't make much money from them. You know, TV, the books, the calendars . . . those are what's paying the piper. Plus, you know, that idiot Riggs kid. If he'd managed to drown himself, there'd be no end of lawsuits. Liability is killing me, gas is up, you name it."

I just nodded. He kept talking, kept not looking at me.

"Besides, you haven't heard the real brainstorm. See, if I convert all this space to my own distribution center, ship the books and calendars and what-have-you from here, then I save an unbelievable amount of money, totally cut out the middle-man."

I nodded, thinking this was what he'd always wanted—to cut out the middleman, the off-to-the-side man, the standing-behind-him man, all men, all women, the people in the town, the man who cooks barbecue, the girl with red hair, the wife who married him, the son who still loved him—all of us, cut out, with nothing left between him and God and money.

"You know, I'll tell you a secret. I might have a line on a weekly TV thing, out of the Glory Network in Charlotte. A show on nutrition and godly living."

I grinned at him. "You're going to need a better haircut," I said.

"You're one to talk, sport," he said. I knew it would always be this, always this jokey way of staying on the surface of things, conversation about sports or weather or the evening news, and I would never really be able to talk to him about the things that mattered to me. I mean, if I couldn't talk to him about Cal, then what could I talk to him about? I remembered he always used to tell me, all the time, that Jesus wanted us to be in the world, but not of it, and that's what he was to me, had made himself—in my world, but not really of it. And standing there, making another joke about haircuts or paperwork or some other thing I've forgotten, I could imagine how it would be, Sunday mornings when I would click the remote and find him on TV, selling his calendars, his books, his daily exercise guides, his T-shirts of boxing-gloves Jesus, how I would watch him, watch his gestures and the fake smile on his face, see right through his fake glasses, and realize that really it wasn't much different this way, seeing him on TV, than it had ever been—I could see him, watch him, study him, but he couldn't see me. And I guessed that he never would.

By noon, my arms are tired, and I'm still trying to figure out why this color of paint should be called Afternoon of a Faun, instead of Yellow, which is what it really is. Painting overhead is the worst, but I do like using the roller, how quick it is. I mean, ten minutes, a whole wall is done. Abel has been griping all week because Mom and Cal are, as they say, "just fixing the place up a little," but really it's more like one of those makeover shows on TV where they give someone a new nose and new teeth and hair and cut away all their fat. Abel keeps saying, "If it ain't broke, don't fix it," and Cal asks him if that saying is part of the Talmud, and Mom says it's not fair to serve food in a place that looks more suited to a wrestling match. I wire in a ceiling fan where he used to have a bare lightbulb, and Mom arranges all these cool-looking wooden school-chairs she's found, and Cal hangs actual curtains for the place while Abel shouts, "You know, people eat with their *fingers* in here."

Just then, Pudge comes tromping up from the basement carrying an armful of soggy cardboard boxes. From the look on his face, he might as well be carrying a dead body he found down there. He doesn't get too far into the room before I realize what he's carrying in those boxes, and I cut my eyes to Cal, who has already cut her eyes to me.

"Hey, Abel?" Pudge says. "You know about these? Pretty serious stuff, black powder and . . . something." He turns his head to read the shipping label. "Potassium chloride and *arsenic*. You got an old lady around here's planning to kill everybody?"

"They're mine," Cal says immediately. "I was planning to use them for stuff. Sorry about that."

Pudge narrows his eyes at her. "Use them for what stuff?" And I know he's not a cop or anything, and I'm happy for a second that Abel isn't friends with Ofc. Toy, but Pudge *does* work as a fireman, has a uniform with official patches all over it, and that's close enough to make me uncomfortable.

"I was going to kill everyone," Cal says, "after I turned old."

"Actually," Abel says, "those have probably been down there forever. Probably there when I bought the building."

Pudge shakes his head. "Naw. Invoice says they got delivered about a month ago. This is dangerous stuff, a fire hazard, and probably illegal. I think we'd better report it."

By now Abel is looking at both of us. He knows. The look on his face is almost too much.

"They're mine," I say, and take a breath. "I use them to make fireworks. I hid them here because I didn't want to get in trouble at the camp."

"I hid them here," Cal says.

"I can't believe you guys would do this," Abel says.

"I asked her to hide them. It's my fault. Abel, I'm really sorry."

He looks at me, saying nothing, then slowly nods. "Confession is good for the soul, Eliot."

"Yeah, unless your mother is standing right behind you," Mom says.

"I still think we need to report these," Pudge says.

"Well, *you'll* have to report them," Abel says. "*We* aren't going to do anything. Pudge, give the kid his boxes and let's get back to work."

Pudge chews on his bottom lip like this is the toughest decision he's ever had to make, then holds out the boxes to me. I look at Cal and start thinking that maybe I'm done with fireworks, at least for now, at least until I can find a way to do it right, without hiding it. Maybe something that beautiful shouldn't be hidden away.

"That's all right," I say. "They're ruined. Throw them in the Dumpster."

That night Abel lets us stay over, Mom on the futon (which is, of all places, in the kitchen) and me on the floor in a sleeping bag, because the next morning Lowe's is delivering the floor sander we've rented, and Mom wants to be right on it first thing. After Mom is asleep I go outside, late, and sit on the porch, waiting for Cal to come downstairs and join me. Finally,

I see her in the dim light from the streetlight, easing closed the screen door, tiptoeing down the stairs. More for show, for herself, I think, because Delores doesn't seem to care much what she does. She's carrying something, and when she gets close I can finally see what, just as she hands it to me—a plate filled with scrambled eggs, toast and jam, bacon, two strawberries.

"I like the strawberries," I tell her.

"Presentation is everything," she says. "I figured we were due another midnight breakfast."

"You mean a last one," I say.

"Eliot, don't."

She sits pressed up next to me, and when I offer her a bite of toast, she shakes her head.

"I'm not going to eat it alone," I say. "That sorta misses the point." She nods, then breaks off a small piece of bacon for herself. In three days, she'll be gone, and I may never see her again. I can't get my head around that idea. My head or my heart. It's like if someone told me that in a week *I* would be gone, not dead, just vanished. Where would I be? Whenever I think about it, my stomach clenches up like a fist, and the panic washes over me like I'm drowning. Some nights I wake up and just say her name, over and over into the dark, like if I never let go of the sound of her name, I will never have to let go of her. Probably fifty times I have told her that I will come see her, that I can take a Greyhound bus and it's cheap, but she always shakes her head, not looking at me. "What's the point?" she asks. She has always been like this when she's sad, like she wants to be pressed to me but also distant, next to me and far away from me at the same time. Like she is practicing being gone. And I don't really get it, how she can turn from me when she's at her most miserable, times when all I want to do is hold her and never let go. It's like the sadness pushes me, pulls her. And her pulling away makes things worse, way worse, for me, but I can't ever tell her that, because then she's even *more* sad, for hurting me. Too many layers of hurt, and it starts to suffocate us both.

She lifts the fork and feeds me a bite of eggs, then a bite of toast. I offer her a bite and she shakes her head.

"I had my ceremonial bite," she says.

"I liked it better when you would just dig in."

She nods, not looking at me. "I haven't been all that hungry lately."

"So you are down to ceremonial bites." I take the plate from my lap and put it behind us on the porch. "You know, I had imagined other kinds of ceremonies for us, other than breakfast in the dark."

"Well, we did have the dance."

I nod. "You were beautiful."

"So were you."

We sit for a while in silence. Some small animal, a cat I think, moves in the grass along Abel's wall, its eyes shining. The air smells like half the town had a cookout that night.

"What kinds of ceremonies?" she says finally.

"Other dances, maybe. Your birthday, my birthday. I just imagined us and time passing, I guess," I say. "Oh, and of course the prom. It's really something at my school, from what I hear. No loud music, no dancing, no public displays of affection. I mean, it's boring, but at least there's nothing to do."

She smiles. "You are one strange guy, Mr. Eliot."

"So, we got to have one ceremony. Out of a thousand."

She turns and looks fully at me. She opens her mouth to speak.

"I know, I know," I say, before she can. "I'll stop."

All week, I have been fighting the math of all of this, of her leaving, knowing that if we were eighteen, it wouldn't make any difference. She could stay, or I could go. I wonder at how thirty-six months can make so much difference; how complicated is the algebra of being in love, when three years can subtract from us the next sixty or seventy. How can that be?

"Eliot," she says, whispering, "I'm as sad as you are."

"Cal . . ." I close my eyes, try to breathe. "You don't *have* to go. Just tell her you aren't. Tell her you're staying."

"Reverse it, Eliot. You go to your parents and say that you aren't staying here anymore, tell them you're moving to New Mexico in three days. Think that'll work?"

Actually I *have* thought about it, pictured it in my head a thousand times, but it's always just some scene from a movie, running away in the dark. The movies never show what happens the next day, when you arrive someplace with nowhere to live, no school to go to, no friends, no parents.

"How about you tell her you are staying just for now, until the restaurant is done. Then we'll figure out the rest?"

She shrugs, frowns. "Now you sound like Abel."

"What do you mean?"

"He has all these plans for me. You know, finish out the year, live in the apartment, work at the Cloven Hoof."

"So? Why not?" My heart starts thudding at the possibility of it.

"Easy. Because you have hopes, Abel has plans, but Delores? Delores has the final say. Delores has the authority. And no matter how crowded the back of the car gets, she hasn't left me behind yet. Even better this time, we get to follow Phi. I get to listen to the Stupid Show at rest stops for two thousand miles."

"Have you even tried?"

"Tried what?"

"Tried saying no. Tried saying 'enough,' tried telling her you're done, no more moving around."

"Well, I have had twenty-three chances in the last four years. Why should twenty-four be any different?"

"Because," I say, "twenty-four is your home."

The next day we spend sanding the floors, and the dust vacuum on the sander doesn't work very well, and by noon we are covered in sweat and the sweat is covered in sawdust. Abel says that it looks like they have finally perfected Shake 'n Bake for humans, and Mom laughs until she can barely breathe.

"It wasn't that funny," I say, with more bite in my words than I meant. Mom looks at me.

"Hey," Abel says, "this is the best audience I ever had, so you hush."

"Why don't you go find her?" Mom says.

"I tried," I tell her. Cal never showed up that morning to work on the restaurant, and twice I have been by to knock on the apartment door, and then I checked the porch, and drove out to the Faire and even out to the camp—all the places she might be, because she loved them or just because she had to be there. Nothing. I go back again and knock at the apartment door, and for a minute I have a panic that they have already gone, that Delores packed them up and made them leave in the middle of the night. According to Cal, it wouldn't be the first time. I even try to reassure myself by peeking in the door and seeing pots still on the stove, her ceramic bowl on the kitchen table, a raincoat draped over the kitchen chair. But even that— most of these moves have been more about what they left behind than what they took, so a ceramic bowl doesn't mean much, other than maybe it didn't fit in the trunk.

By nine that night I'm frantic, and even Mom and Abel head out in his truck to look. By ten we have given up and I don't know what to do. I keep going to the window and pulling the curtain to the side, and then sitting on the couch in the dark and staring at my hands. Those two things seem to be all I can manage, and I wonder if it will be that way forever. Right now it's hard to imagine I ever could manage more than looking out or looking down, looking at the emptiness of my hands, and sometimes saying her name.

Near eleven I look out for maybe the twentieth time, and something is different, like a *What's Wrong with This Picture?* puzzle, and it takes me a minute to realize that the tiny light in the apartment window, the one above the sink, is on, shining into the dark, and just as I start to turn and shout to Mom and Abel, I see a shape on the porch and realize that it's Cal, just sitting there in the dark. In two seconds I am out the door.

"Where the hell have you been?" I say.

"I'm fine, thanks, and you?"

"Cal . . ." I move to sit beside her.

She shakes her head. Already enough hair has grown back that it moves a teeny when she does that. "I was walking around. Everywhere. All day."

"I looked for you."

"I know. Twice I saw you drive past, like two blocks away from me."

"Well, you could have—"

"Eliot, I came by here to tell you good-bye."

My heart freezes inside my chest, and then it feels like all this heat gathers around it, burning me in the middle. "I . . . you have two days left," I tell her.

She tilts her face up toward the streetlight, and tears shine along her cheeks, though she's not making any crying noises. I reach out, as softly as I can, and brush away her tears with the side of my thumb. "We'll be packing, arguing most likely," she says. "I don't want you to see me like that, jamming my life into the back of a Datsun. Just . . . let this be it, okay?"

I nod, then shake my head. I take her head in my hands and turn her to me, holding her there, cupping her in my hands, taking her in with my eyes, trying to fall into her, my fingers lightly shaking in her hair, and I know that tomorrow when my hands are empty again, that emptiness will engulf me, surround me in silence, and I will fall into that instead, into emptiness and nothing. "Cal . . ." I say. "My Calliope . . ." And my own tears rim and quiver at the edges of my vision, blurring her, finally falling when she leans in to kiss me, just pressing her lips to mine and holding them there.

"I want you to wear this," she says, and slips something into my hand. When I look down it's her bottle cap. It's the first time I have really looked at it, and I have to tilt it in the light to do so. The cap is bent in the middle, woven all around with strands of glass thread. "Someone else I love gave that to me," she says. "I like it, because it makes me think that you can take the most regular, ordinary thing and make it beautiful. I think that's what we did."

"I think so too. And I think it would be terrible if something came along and destroyed this. It should last forever."

She takes the red string from my fingers, lifts it to place it around my neck.

"Yeah, it should," she says. "But it won't. That's just how things are."

I nod, but as she slips it inside my T-shirt and I can feel it cold against my skin, I know that she's wrong. I will keep it forever, take care of it, and never ever let it break.

calliope 17

It was the sight of the boxes that set me off. Three boxes labeled: KEEP, TOSS, DISCUSS. I knew that it was Delores's way of pretending that there was actually room to talk, to have a conversation, to express my views. I took the black Sharpie and relabeled the boxes, giving them their real names. KEEP, TOSS, TALK ABOUT BUT STILL TOSS. I looked at the KEEP box, a carton that had once held boxes of Rice Krispies but was now supposed to hold my life. If Eliot were here maybe I would laugh that my life is really *part of this nutritious breakfast.* I tried to imagine my life on a table with juice and a piece of toast and an apple and wondered if that was how Delores thought of me, as an add-on, as something to be compensated for, as something without nutritional value, unnecessary. I might laugh about this with Eliot, but then again, maybe not. Maybe some things aren't funny no matter how you try to talk about them.

I've nearly gone over there a million times today. I know he's there, only a few blocks from here, the closest he will be for a long time, maybe ever, but I stop myself every time. No sense making it worse, letting him see me like this. I know it hurts him when I pull away from him, but what can I do? I can't stay close, knowing that it's my closeness that hurts him. Knowing that I am the one that puts the sadness in his eyes. He tells me that if he didn't love me so much, it wouldn't be so hard. Sometimes it makes me wish he didn't, didn't love me so much, so that it didn't hurt him. So that he could just move on, away from me.

I place a shoe box in the bottom of the KEEP box, sliding it into the corner, where I cover it with a folded beach towel with CAROLINA BEACH painted across it in rainbow letters. I know I have to hide things like this. Delores would never understand. She would never understand the significance of a receipt for two ice-cream cones, or half an eggshell, cleaned and dried so that it glows like porcelain. How could she understand why I would want to keep an empty cellophane bag that once held chocolate chips or a burned cylinder that took me two hours of walking around in the woods to find? How could I expect that she would want to take up the precious space in her hatchback with a dried corsage or with a balloon that once hung from the rafters of a cafeteria decorated to look like the South Seas?

On top of the towel I place a menu that I took from the Cloven Hoof and a jar of barbecue sauce that Abel swears is the hottest that he has ever made. Cal's Fury is what he called it.

"I've never seen you mad, but I suspect when you are, you burn everything you touch, like this sauce." He handed it to me on the back porch of his house. "Don't keep it long," he told me. "It'll go bad if you don't use it." Always instructing me in the ways of life, even with a jar of barbecue sauce.

"We're leaving early," I told him.

"I thought as much," he said, shifting his eyes to look at the sky behind me.

"I don't want you getting up in the morning to say good-bye," I said, staring down at my feet. "You need your sleep." He sighed deeply, but didn't say anything. I looked up to see him staring at me. We stood like that for a few moments, before I looked away. "I guess I should go pack," I said, turning toward the driveway.

"Cal," he said, touching my arm with his fingertips. I turned back to look at him, but he didn't say anything else. He just looked at me for a moment before closing his eyes and nodding. I left him standing there on his back porch, watching the sky as it slowly faded from bright blue to navy, then black. He was still standing there even as the stars were beginning to shine through the darkness, like holes to heaven.

He must have gone inside since I started packing my box, because the porch is empty and a light is shining in his kitchen, bright against the darkness of the night. I hear the sound of tires on the driveway and hold my breath, listening, hoping to hear the squeak of the shocks on Linda's van or the rumbling growl of Abel's truck. Instead I hear the familiar pop of Delores's Datsun as she shifts it into park. My stomach flips over once as I hear the thunk of her boots on the steps and then the whine of the screen door as she pulls it open. I don't turn to look at her as she enters, but I can still feel her there, feel the familiar frantic energy that she carries with her wherever she goes, like a caged animal, looking for a way out.

"Good. I was hoping that you would have started already," she says from behind me. She walks up behind me, nearly burning me with her heat. "How's it going?" she asks, peering into the TOSS box. I can feel her frown, seeing it empty. She steps back and reads the words that I have printed on the last box and makes a clucking noise with her mouth. She turns the box with the toe of her boot so that the lettering is against the wall. If she can't see my unhappiness, it doesn't exist.

I walk past her and to the kitchen table, lifting Abel's bowl from the table. I carry it over to where I am working and lay it in the center of his raincoat, folding the arms around the bowl to cushion it before lifting it into my box. I place it carefully, tucking T-shirts around it to protect it.

"Oh, Cal," Delores says, watching me. "No." I stand and turn toward her, feeling every one of the nearly eight inches I have on her. I try half a dozen responses before I settle on one.

"Yes," I say, watching her face. "See, this is the KEEP box. This one's not open for discussion."

"Don't start with me," she says, lifting her chin. "I don't want to hear it." She starts to turn away from me and walk into the bedroom. I actually laugh out loud when she says that, making her turn back to face me. "I didn't realize I was being funny."

"Oh, but you are," I say, still smiling. "Funny, I mean. Because I think the thing is even if I do say it, it's not like you are going to hear it, so I might as well say whatever I like."

"I have always listened to you," she says, narrowing her eyes, and I can tell that I have gone too far, but I don't stop.

"You have *never* listened to me," I say, and now I'm not laughing at all. My face is hard, my mouth a firm line. "The thing is, Delores," I say, stuffing my hands into my pockets, "maybe it's not even your fault." This startles her and I see her eyes soften a bit.

"What's not my fault?" she asks.

"Maybe it's not totally your fault that you've never listened to me." I look past her and take a deep breath. "Maybe it's just as much my fault because I've never really told you."

"Never really told me what?"

"Never told you that I don't want to go."

"You don't want to go to New Mexico," she says, trying to keep her voice even.

"I don't want to go anywhere. I want to stay here." I let out a breath that I feel like I have been holding for over four years, feeling it curl out of my lungs and through my lips into the air. It's Delores's turn to try on responses. I see her mind working as she fashions each one and discards it, in favor of the next.

When she finally says something, it's flat, featureless, practiced, not only by her, but by thousands of parents over the years. Unfortunately, from her it fails even more than usual.

"I am your mother," she says, softly but with force. "You will do as I say." Her voice builds as her confidence grows. "And what I say is that you will pack your things or I will pack them for you. In the morning, you will get yourself in the car. Is that understood?"

"I have no say in this?"

"None," she says, starting to turn toward the bedroom again, apparently confident that she has instructed me in my role as the quiet daughter with no opinions, no feelings, no dreams. She stops and turns back toward me. "Are we clear?" she asks, as if remembering that she hasn't used every cliché that a parent can trot out to talk to her child.

"It's amazing," I say. "You look like a mother, you talk like a mother, you even sometimes act like a mother, but you're missing one crucial thing."

"And just what would that be?" she asks. Her eyes are flashing now and I feel the heat pouring off her, consuming me, making my head spin.

"Love," I say, and it's as if that one word is a fountain of water splashing over both of us. Her anger sputters and flares against the spray, fighting for life before it goes out. She stands before me soaked, limp, drowned. She walks past me, grabbing at the sweater that still hangs on the hook by the door, yanking it down. I hear the screen door squeak, then slam, then the sounds of her footsteps walking away from me. An engine growls to life and tires crunch on the driveway before going quiet. Sounds that are so familiar after all these years. The sounds of pulling away, retreating, leaving, abandoning.

I am suddenly tired. I feel like I can't even remember a time when I wasn't tired, as if my whole life has been one long period of awareness, wakefulness, vigilance. As if for the first time that I can remember I can relax, sleep, rest. I lie down on the bed and close my eyes, listening to the sound of the cicadas calling to one another in the trees and the sound of the wind as it nestles into the eaves, rocking the room gently as if to a lullaby that has all but been forgotten by the world.

Once upon a time, in a land far, far away, there lived a beautiful princess in a wondrous castle made of alabaster and crystal. She lived her days happily doing what most princesses do. She spent her time traveling the countryside in her exquisite golden chariot; studying science, music, and literature; and creating works of art in her private studio. During the afternoons, she would stroll the palace grounds, granting an audience to her royal subjects and admiring the beauty that lay all around her. Each evening she would dine with her parents, the queen and king, when they would discuss the happenings of the day and their dreams for the future. At night the king and queen would tuck her into her feather bed, all covered in silk and velvet, and kiss her good night, watching as she drifted off to sleep. All was well within the kingdom.

Until one day.

A time came when she began to see cracks in the crystal palace and notice rips in the tapestries that hung from the walls. She watched as the trees in the garden, which had once been heavy with fruit and flowers, began to wither and fade. The queen would disappear for days at a time, slipping away to places unknown, until she would return, pale and broken, pulled in on herself. One day the princess's chariot stopped sparkling, and the next day her horses disappeared. The colors in her paints began to fade and dry. Books began to crumble to dust and food spoiled before they could eat it. Even the king and queen seemed to grow fainter, shrinking in upon themselves. Where there was once singing and laughter, now there was silence.

The princess suspected some dark spell had been cast upon the palace and set about to find its source. She scoured their books for magic that might counteract the curse. She lay awake at night trying to discover the secret of the evil power. She took to carrying charms and saying prayers to ward off the darkness.

On a day wet with the tears of heaven, the queen announced that they would leave the cursed kingdom in search of another land, where they might find happiness and peace once again. She began to pack their belongings into her own chariot. This one was blue as the sapphire sea. As the princess watched, trunks full of the royal jewels, bags full of gowns and robes, and boxes full of books were placed in the chariot. She kept watching as the chariot was filled with their things, wondering where the king might put his belongings. In another chariot perhaps? But there was none, only the golden one that lay broken in the dying fields.

A king must never leave his kingdom, he explained. On the last night, the princess heard the king asking the queen to stay, but the proud and beautiful queen never changed her mind. Late in the night the king came to the princess, calling her from her bed and leading her into the kitchen. There he had prepared a feast, which they ate in silence, holding hands in the wan light. The princess had never known the king to cry, but there in the darkness, she could see the tears coursing down his cheeks, sparkling like rivers of diamonds.

The day of their journey dawned, wet and bleak. The whole kingdom was dark with mourning. As the king helped the princess into the chariot, he looked at his queen, but she would not turn her eyes to him. "Please never forget," the king told the princess, pressing a silvery talisman into her palm before closing the door. As the queen urged the horses onto the road, the princess looked at the folded circle in her hand. It was a gift, one that might keep her safe, one that she must never lose, one that would help her find her way. As the chariot sped forward into the countryside, she knew that she might never know a home again. She folded her fingers over the talisman, whispering a prayer that it wouldn't be true.

Often it's the sudden silence that wakes you from sleep. You get used to the noises of boxes being lifted and floor planks creaking. The sounds of the toilet flushing and the water running become the sound track of your dreams. Eggs frying, toast popping, even a door slamming become the circadian rhythms that keep your eyes closed and your breathing deep. It's when it gets quiet, so quiet that the absence of sound becomes too noisy, that you wake.

Sometimes it's the intensity of someone watching you, looking at you, that draws you from your dreams. It's as if even with your eyes closed you can feel someone watching you, thinking, wondering. Maybe it's a primal mechanism that keeps you from harm, or maybe it's less ancient and instead is the way your consciousness is linked to someone else's.

This morning it was both.

I opened my eyes to see Delores standing over me, watching me. She reached down as if to tuck my hair behind my ear, as if she had forgotten that it wasn't there, but her fingers stroked my cheek instead, so softly that I could barely feel it and wondered if I were still dreaming. She smiled at me, that faraway smile, that pulled-back smile. The smile that she had taught me meant she was leaving or maybe had already left. Then she bent and brushed my cheek with her lips, the first time I can remember her kissing me in years, maybe ever. It was always me that kissed her, feeling her body stiffen under my touch. Her lips felt dry and soft against my skin and I closed my eyes, memorizing the place, the sound, the touch. "I'll see you soon," she whispered. I kept my eyes closed, afraid to see her walking away, afraid to see her leaving. I listened as two engines started in the driveway, one familiar, the other not. I kept listening to the crunch of tires on the gravel, the bump at the end of the driveway, and then the acceleration onto the street. I kept listening until all I heard was silence, so loud that I couldn't hear anything else.

It was a long time before I could lift myself out of bed, before I could walk to the window and see the emptiness of the driveway, but now I am standing here, looking around at my things, my place, my apartment. I'm looking at my home. Suddenly the space seems too small to hold me and I have to walk outside, walk down the steps, walk across the driveway, around the corner, and up the street. I walk up onto the porch, hearing the music and a power drill and the sound of a woman talking. I walk through the doorway and toward the kitchen, where I know they will be. Abel is leaning against the sink, a cup of coffee in his hands, blowing across it as I have seen him do hundreds of times. Linda is kneeling on the counter, mounting shelves to hold mixing bowls and spices and measuring cups. Eliot is steadying the end of the shelf, his arms overhead, his face turned upward. I wait for Linda to finish securing the shelf before I speak.

"Hi," I say. "What can I do?"

It took some doing—and I mean a solid month of work—but we finally have all the paddleboats installed in the restaurant. This went along with Mom's idea to open up the back storage room of the Cloven Hoof to double Abel's capacity for seating customers, and to turn the basement into the storage area instead. I remember the night she came up with all of this. She looked around at all our new paint and drywall and curtains and lights, and shook her head.

"I swear, Abel," she said, "there are about fifty ways you could make this place run better, make more money, I mean—" She looked suddenly like someone had slapped her. "Abel, I'm *sorry*," she said. "Old habits die hard, I guess. You probably don't care about making more money."

He took off his hat long enough to scratch his head and nod, pretending to be all depressed. "Awful, horrible stuff," he said, shaking his head at Cal and me. "Every day, I wish some kind soul would come in here and rob me at gunpoint."

We had just gotten ourselves Cokes from Abel's cooler and were sitting around, the four of us, in dusty clothes, five weeks from the grand reopening. "You know what I mean," Mom said. "I don't want to get caught up in *that* again. But, well . . ." She looked around again. "I'm just saying."

"Then just say. Tell me how to wring another dollar out of the place. That one there is going to need school clothes." He pointed at Cal, who squeezed my hand. She had talked me into staying at Lighthouse Academy, and would join me there in September for our junior year. She told me we'd be big fish in a small pond, then made that smirk that scrunches up her nose. "Small baptismal pool, I mean," she said. "I guess I better learn the lingo, huh?" But Abel wasn't paying for everything. She got money from her dad, now that she had a permanent address, and he has planned to come see her at Thanksgiving, when, Abel promised, we would deep-fry our turkey. He told her that you couldn't invite a Texan to North Carolina and not deep-fry something, and told me that I would enjoy it because it was likely the whole thing would go up in flames.

Besides the money her father sent, every week without fail an envelope came from Delores, sometimes containing five dollars, sometimes twenty-five. And always a note. The cool thing was, she was sending Cal a letter by enclosing just one word each week. The first week, Cal was like, *what?* because she got this

piece of paper with a big *I* written on it and ten bucks folded
inside, from Santa Fe. The next week was fifteen dollars and
MISS, and then five dollars and *YOU*. Cal said in ways it was
the best communication she'd ever had from her mom. This
month already she'd gotten money with notes saying *WE, ARE,
HAVING*.

"The next few had better say 'a good time,'" Cal said,
"because if it says 'a baby,' I am going to *freak* out." The next
week she got a *SUCH*. All the notes went up on her refrigerator.

After Abel asked about squeezing more money out of the
place, Mom told him her idea for making the place bigger, and
for the boats. "And," she told him, "you should rent the space
upstairs to me and this young man"—she pointed at me—"and
stop letting us sleep on your floor for free."

"You drive a hard bargain, but okay. You can give me money.
Then again, if you both are working here, at the restaurant,
shouldn't I just give myself the money?"

"Nah," she said. "I want to hold it, just for a little bit." They
both laughed.

Abel seemed willing to do anything she said, and a week later
we started bringing in the paddleboats, which The Dad had
sold to her when he auctioned off most of the camp equipment
to raise money for his new TV show, *Bread of Life*.

We pulled out the gears and the pedals, stripped the boats
down to just the Fiberglas shells, mounted them to the floor in
the back room, and bolted tabletops to the boats. Couples sit in

them to eat, like little plastic love seats, Mom said, a booth for just two. There are oars and life preservers on the walls, a lake mural painted on the wall. It's pretty popular, and people call up and reserve the red boat or the green one, or the one by the back window. Mom put Riggs's yellow boat where, she said, she could keep an eye on it. And the one by the back window? That's ours, the blue boat that Cal and I took out on the lake that night.

The Grand Reopening of the Cloven Hoof was two weeks ago, and there was even a story in the paper about the flood and the paddleboats and the expanded menu. My barbecue sauce and the one Abel had named for Cal are now both on the menu. Cal said we should be proud, that it wasn't every high school student whose name was immortalized in laminated cardboard.

My favorite time to work is Sunday night, because the restaurant is closed on Mondays, and Cal and I send Mom upstairs and Abel down the street so we can finish the cleanup, or sometimes the two of them walk down the block for ice cream. One ice-cream cone equals one mile of jogging is Mom's rule, and Abel abides by it. Tonight, like the other Sunday nights, Cal and I turn the dead bolt in the front door, flip the sign in the window to CLOSED, turn off the music that runs in through the speakers, and work in near silence, bussing the tables, loading the dishwasher, putting everything away.

When we finish, Cal pulls off her apron over her head, rubs

at the stains on her T-shirt, and turns off the last of the lights. I put our dirty aprons in the laundry bag, then walk up behind her, slip my hands around her waist. Already her hair is back down to the top of her shirt collar, and I press my face into it, breathe her in, still not believing sometimes that she is here. She holds my arms and leans back against me, letting her weight fall into me, my chin on her shoulder.

"Our last Sunday night before school starts," she says. "Kinda weird."

"Well, not too much will change, we'll still work here, still have our Sunday nights."

I can feel her face move beside mine as she smiles. "They'll be school nights," she says. "You know, I'm a little bit freaked out."

"Why? Don't be."

"What if they think I'm a heathen?"

I tighten my arms around her. "Are you?"

"I don't know. I'll get back to you after my first heathen seminar." She turns her head to kiss the side of my face. Outside, a late summer rain dots the glass of the window.

"Well, listen," I tell her. "I'll make sure everyone is nice to you."

"And your word carries a lot of weight around there, huh?"

"Are you kidding? Have you met me?"

She laughs and slips out of my arms, then takes my hand and moves us to the back room. We find our blue paddleboat and slide across it in the dark, slipping down in the seat under the tall back window. This has become our tradition, every Sunday night after closing, for the last three Sundays, sitting here, holding each other, not saying much and not needing to. It is, Cal says, our first tradition, and I will find out in the months ahead how much she loves all traditions, simply because she has never really had them—we will carve the deep-fried turkey, and bake pumpkin pies, and cut out jack-o'-lanterns, and lie on the floor in the dark on Christmas Eve, looking up through the branches of lights in the tree, as if at a field of stars. But she likes this one best, she tells me, because it's ours alone. Sunday-night-indoor-paddleboat sitting has not caught on with many people. But here we are, breathing each other's breath, kissing, my fingers in her hair, and then she settles in against me, pressing tight, hooking her leg over mine. We watch the streaks of rain gather on the glass and slip down in tiny rivers, listen to the sound it makes on the panes, on the roof far above us. The best part of these Sunday nights in the boat is when the sky is cloudless, and if we are there on the right night and wait long enough, the moonlight shines in through the window and settles over us in the dark, filling up the floor of the boat just like it did that first night. Only it's different now. We don't have to move, don't have to paddle anywhere. We stay where we are, and the moon finds us.